The Man Who Was Kipling

Ruskin Bond has been writing for over sixty years, and now has over 120 titles in print—novels, collections of short stories, poetry, essays, anthologies and books for children. His first novel, *The Room on the Roof*, received the prestigious John Llewellyn Rhys Prize in 1957. He has also received the Padma Shri (1999), the Padma Bhushan (2014) and two awards from Sahitya Akademi—one for his short stories and another for his writings for children. In 2012, the Delhi government gave him its Lifetime Achievement Award.

Born in 1934, Ruskin Bond grew up in Jamnagar, Shimla, New Delhi and Dehradun. Apart from three years in the UK, he has spent all his life in India, and now lives in Mussoorie with his adopted family.

RUSKIN BOND

The Man Who Was Kipling

Published by
Rupa Publications India Pvt. Ltd 2017
7/16, Ansari Road, Daryaganj
New Delhi 110002

Sales centres:
Allahabad Bengaluru Chennai
Hyderabad Jaipur Kathmandu
Kolkata Mumbai

Copyright © Ruskin Bond 2017

This is a work of fiction. Names, characters, places and incidents are either the product of the author's imagination or are used fictitiously and any resemblance to any actual person, living or dead, events or locales is entirely coincidental.

All rights reserved.
No part of this publication may be reproduced, transmitted, or stored in a retrieval system, in any form or by any means, electronic, mechanical, photocopying, recording or otherwise, without the prior permission of the publisher.

ISBN: 978-81-291-4851-3

First impression 2017

10 9 8 7 6 5 4 3 2 1

Printed at Parksons Graphics Pvt. Ltd. Mumbai

This book is sold subject to the condition that it shall not, by way of trade or otherwise, be lent, resold, hired out, or otherwise circulated, without the publisher's prior consent, in any form of binding or cover other than that in which it is published.

CONTENTS

Introduction	vii
The Woman on Platform No. 8	1
The Man Who Was Kipling	7
Death of a Familiar	12
A Case for Inspector Lal	30
The Bent-Double Beggar	39
The Story of Madhu	47
All Creatures Great and Small	52
A Love of Long Ago	67
The Bar that Time Forgot	73
The Last Tonga Ride	87
Calypso Christmas	102
Sita and the River	107

INTRODUCTION

Writing comes naturally to me. And writing about the people and places I have known and the paths that I have taken comes even more easily. Having lived in London, Delhi, Dehradun and Mussoorie, it is these places that often feature in my stories. Though differing in their pace, both cities and towns have given me equally great stories.

Do you know about the time I was in the Victoria and Albert Museum in London and met none other than Rudyard Kipling? I assure you I wasn't dreaming (at least I hope I wasn't). He looked exactly as he does in the pictures: that heavy moustache and those horn-rimmed spectacles. We had a long chat about *Kim*, and then he wanted to know about the status of the Grand Trunk Road. It was truly a fan moment for me, even if it was only his ghost!

I have collected a few of such stories that take you back to simple and unspoilt times. These twelve pieces of fiction will take you on a ride through romance, mystery, friendship, horror, courage and the warmth of human relationships.

Some stories have such wise, affectionate, colourful and

charismatic characters that they will stay with the reader long after he is finished with the book. There is Arun, a schoolboy, who is befriended by an unknown woman while waiting at a railway station. An English-speaking beggar named Ganpat, who can recite passages from Shakespeare. A handsome and cocksure young man, Sunil, who meets a tragic end due to his philandering ways. Seventeen-year-old Kamla with sparkling brown eyes and a laughing, mischievous face, always ready to break into a smile or peals of laughter. A happy-go-lucky West Indian boy called George who comes to London in search of better prospects, but gets baffled by how devoid of colour, music and sunshine London can be. Sita, a ten-year-old girl who survives an angry river and devastating rains through pure courage and faith in the gods.

There are many more stories to be told and characters to be remembered. But there will be time for them later. For now I have put together this collection to entertain you. May it be a rewarding read for you, my beloved readers.

Ruskin Bond

THE WOMAN ON PLATFORM NO. 8

It was my second year at boarding school, and I was sitting on platform no. 8 at Ambala station, waiting for the northern bound train. I think I was about twelve at the time. My parents considered me old enough to travel alone, and I had arrived by bus at Ambala early in the evening; now there was a wait till midnight before my train arrived. Most of the time I had been pacing up and down the platform, browsing through the bookstall, or feeding broken biscuits to stray dogs; trains came and went, the platform would be quiet for a while and then, when a train arrived, it would be an inferno of heaving, shouting, agitated human bodies. As the carriage doors opened, a tide of people would sweep down upon the nervous little ticket collector at the gate; and every time this happened I would be caught in the rush and swept outside the station. Now tired of this game and of ambling about the platform, I sat down on my suitcase and gazed dismally across the railway tracks.

Trolleys rolled past me, and I was conscious of the cries of the various vendors—the men who sold curds and lemon, the sweetmeat seller, the newspaper boy—but I had lost interest in all that was going on along the busy platform, and continued to stare across the railway tracks, feeling bored and a little lonely.

'Are you all alone, my son?' asked a soft voice close behind me.

I looked up and saw a woman standing near me. She was leaning over, and I saw a pale face and dark kind eyes. She wore no jewels, and was dressed very simply in a white sari.

'Yes, I am going to school,' I said, and stood up respectfully. She seemed poor, but there was a dignity about her that commanded respect.

'I have been watching you for some time,' she said. 'Didn't your parents come to see you off?'

'I don't live here,' I said. 'I had to change trains. Anyway, I can travel alone.'

'I am sure you can,' she said, and I liked her for saying that, and I also liked her for the simplicity of her dress, and for her deep, soft voice and the serenity of her face.

'Tell me, what is your name?' she asked.

'Arun,' I said.

'And how long do you have to wait for your train?'

'About an hour, I think. It comes at twelve o' clock.'

'Then come with me and have something to eat.'

I was going to refuse, out of shyness and suspicion, but she took me by the hand, and then I felt it would be silly to pull my hand away. She told a coolie to look after my suitcase, and then she led me away down the platform. Her hand was gentle, and she held mine neither too firmly nor too lightly. I looked up at her again. She was not young. And she was not old. She must have been over thirty, but had she been fifty, I think she would have looked much the same.

She took me into the station dining room, ordered tea and samosas and jalebis, and at once I began to thaw and take a new interest in this kind woman. The strange encounter had little effect on my appetite. I was a hungry schoolboy, and I ate as much as I could in as polite a manner as possible. She took obvious pleasure in watching me eat, and I think it was the food that strengthened the bond between us and cemented our friendship, for under the influence of the tea and sweets I began to talk quite freely, and told her about my school, my friends, my likes and dislikes. She questioned me quietly from time to time, but preferred listening; she drew me out very well, and I had soon forgotten that we were strangers. But she did not ask me about my family or where I lived, and I did not ask her where she lived. I accepted her for what she had been to me—a quiet, kind and gentle woman who gave sweets to a lonely boy on a railway platform…

After about half an hour we left the dining room and began walking back along the platform. An engine was shunting up and down beside platform no. 8, and as it approached, a boy leapt off the platform and ran across the rails, taking a short cut to the next platform. He was at a safe distance from the engine, but as he leapt across the rails, the woman clutched my arm. Her fingers dug into my flesh, and I winced with pain. I caught her fingers and looked up at her, and I saw a spasm of pain and fear and sadness pass across her face. She watched the boy as he climbed the platform, and it was not until he had disappeared into the crowd that she relaxed her hold on my arm. She smiled at me reassuringly and took my hand again, but her fingers trembled against mine.

'He was all right,' I said, feeling that it was she who needed reassurance.

She smiled gratefully at me and pressed my hand. We walked together in silence until we reached the place where I had left my suitcase. One of my schoolfellows, Satish, a boy of about my age, had turned up with his mother.

'Hello, Arun!' he called. 'The train's coming in late, as usual. Did you know we have a new headmaster this year?'

We shook hands, and then he turned to his mother and said: 'This is Arun, Mother. He is one of my friends, and the best bowler in the class.'

'I am glad to know that,' said his mother, a large imposing woman who wore spectacles. She looked at the woman who held my hand and said: 'And I suppose you're Arun's mother?'

I opened my mouth to give some explanation, but before I could say anything the woman replied: 'Yes, I am Arun's mother.'

I was unable to speak a word. I looked quickly up at the woman, but she did not appear to be at all embarrassed, and was smiling at Satish's mother.

Satish's mother said: 'It's such a nuisance having to wait for the train right in the middle of the night. But one can't let the child wait here alone. Anything can happen to a boy at a big station like this—there are so many suspicious characters hanging about. These days one has to be very careful of strangers.'

'Arun can travel alone though,' said the woman beside me, and somehow I felt grateful to her for saying that. I had already forgiven her for lying; and besides, I had taken an instinctive dislike to Satish's mother.

'Well, be very careful, Arun,' said Satish's mother looking sternly at me through her spectacles. 'Be very careful when your mother is not with you. And never talk to strangers!'

I looked from Satish's mother to the woman who had given me tea and sweets, and back at Satish's mother.

'I like strangers,' I said.

Satish's mother definitely staggered a little, as obviously she was not used to being contradicted by young boys. 'There you are, you see! If you don't watch over them all the time, they'll walk straight into trouble. Always listen to what your mother tells you,' she said, wagging a fat little finger at me. 'And never, never talk to strangers.'

I glared resentfully at her, and moved closer to the woman who had befriended me. Satish was standing behind his mother, grinning at me, and delighting in my clash with his mother. Apparently, he was on my side.

The station bell clanged, and the people who had till now been squatting resignedly on the platform began bustling about.

'Here it comes,' shouted Satish, as the engine whistle shrieked and the front lights played over the rails.

The train moved slowly into the station, the engine hissing and sending out waves of steam. As it came to a stop, Satish jumped on the footboard of a lighted compartment and shouted, 'Come on, Arun, this one's empty!' and I picked up my suitcase and made a dash for the open door.

We placed ourselves at the open windows, and the two women stood outside on the platform, talking up to us. Satish's mother did most of the talking.

'Now don't jump on and off moving trains, as you did

just now,' she said. 'And don't stick your heads out of the windows, and don't eat any rubbish on the way.' She allowed me to share the benefit of her advice, as she probably didn't think my 'mother' a very capable person. She handed Satish a bag of fruit, a cricket bat and a big box of chocolates, and told him to share the food with me. Then she stood back from the window to watch how my 'mother' behaved.

I was smarting under the patronizing tone of Satish's mother, who obviously thought mine a very poor family; and I did not intend giving the other woman away. I let her take my hand in hers, but I could think of nothing to say. I was conscious of Satish's mother staring at us with hard, beady eyes, and I found myself hating her with a firm, unreasoning hate. The guard walked up the platform, blowing his whistle for the train to leave. I looked straight into the eyes of the woman who held my hand, and she smiled in a gentle, understanding way. I leaned out of the window then, and put my lips to her cheek and kissed her.

The carriage jolted forward, and she drew her hand away.

'Goodbye, Mother!' said Satish, as the train began to move slowly out of the station. Satish and his mother waved at each other.

'Goodbye,' I said to the other woman, 'goodbye—Mother...' I didn't wave or shout, but sat still in front of the window, gazing at the woman on the platform. Satish's mother was talking to her, but she didn't appear to be listening; she was looking at me, as the train took me away. She stood there on the busy platform, a pale sweet woman in white, and I watched her until she was lost in the milling crowd.

THE MAN WHO WAS KIPLING

I was sitting on a bench in the Indian Section of the Victoria and Albert Museum in London, when a tall, stooping, elderly gentleman sat down beside me. I gave him a quick glance, noting his swarthy features, heavy moustache and horn-rimmed spectacles. There was something familiar and disturbing about his face, and I couldn't resist looking at him again.

I noticed that he was smiling at me.

'Do you recognize me?' he asked, in a soft pleasant voice.

'Well, you do seem familiar,' I said. 'Haven't we met somewhere?'

'Perhaps. But if I seem familiar to you, that is at least something. The trouble these days is that people don't *know* me anymore—I'm a familiar, that's all. Just a name standing for a lot of outmoded ideas.'

A little perplexed, I asked, 'What is it you do?'

'I wrote books once. Poems and tales... Tell me, whose books do you read?'

'Oh, Maugham, Priestley, Thurber. And among the older lot, Bennett and Wells—.' I hesitated, groping for an important name, and I noticed a shadow, a sad shadow, pass across my companion's face.

'Oh, yes, and Kipling,' I said. 'I read a lot of Kipling.'

His face brightened up at once, and the eyes behind the thick-lensed spectacles suddenly came to life.

'I'm Kipling,' he said.

I stared at him in astonishment, and then, realizing that he might perhaps be dangerous, I smiled feebly and said, 'Oh, yes?'

'You probably don't believe me. I'm dead, of course.'

'So I thought.'

'And you don't believe in ghosts?'

'Not as a rule.'

'But you'd have no objection to talking to one, if he came along?'

'I'd have no objection. But how do I know you're Kipling? How do I know you're not an imposter?'

'Listen, then:

> When my heavens were turned to blood,
> When the dark had filled my day,
> Furthest, but most faithful, stood
> That lone star I cast away.
> I had loved myself, and I
> Have not lived and dare not die.'

'Once,' he said, gripping me by the arm and looking me straight in the eye. 'Once in life I watched a star; but I whistled her to go.'

'Your star hasn't fallen yet,' I said, suddenly moved, suddenly quite certain that I sat beside Kipling. 'One day, when there is a new spirit of adventure abroad, we will discover you again.'

'Why have they heaped scorn on me for so long?'

'You were too militant, I suppose—too much of an Empire man. You were too patriotic for your own good.'

He looked a little hurt. 'I was never very political,' he said. 'I wrote over six hundred poems, and you could only call a dozen of them political, I have been abused for harping on the theme of the White Man's Burden but my only aim was to show off the Empire to my audience—and I believed the Empire was a fine and noble thing. Is it wrong to believe in something? I never went deeply into political issues, that's true. You must remember, my seven years in India were very youthful years. I was in my twenties, a little immature if you like, and my interest in India was a boy's interest. Action appealed to me more than anything else. You must understand that.'

'No one has described action more vividly, or India so well. I feel at one with Kim wherever he goes along the Grand Trunk Road, in the temples at Banaras, amongst the Saharanpur fruit gardens, on the snow-covered Himalayas. Kim has colour and movement and poetry.'

He sighed, and a wistful look came into his eyes.

'I'm prejudiced, of course,' I continued. 'I've spent most of my life in India—not *your* India, but an India that does still have much of the colour and atmosphere that you captured. You know, Mr Kipling, you can still sit in a third-class railway carriage and meet the most wonderful assortment of people. In any village you will still find the same courtesy, dignity and courage that the Lama and Kim found on their travels.'

'And the Grand Trunk Road? Is it still a long winding procession of humanity?'

'Well, not exactly,' I said, a little ruefully. 'It's just a procession of motor vehicles now. The poor Lama would be run down by a truck if he became too dreamy on the Grand Trunk Road. Times *have* changed. There are no more Mrs Hawksbees in Simla, for instance.'

There was a faraway look in Kipling's eyes. Perhaps he was imagining himself a boy again; perhaps he could see the hills or the red dust of Rajputana; perhaps he was having a private conversation with Privates Mulvaney and Ortheris, or perhaps he was out hunting with the Seonce wolf pack. The sound of London's traffic came to us through the glass doors, but we heard only the creaking of bullock-cart wheels and the distant music of a flute.

He was talking to himself, repeating a passage from one of his stories. 'And the last puff of the day wind brought from the unseen villages the scent of damp woodsmoke, hot cakes, dripping undergrowth, and rotting pine cones. That is the true smell of the Himalayas, and if once it creeps into the blood of a man, that man will at the last, forgetting all else, return to the hills to die.'

A mist seemed to have risen between us—or had it come in from the streets?—and when it cleared, Kipling had gone away.

I asked the gatekeeper if he had seen a tall man with a slight stoop, wearing spectacles.

'Nope,' said the gatekeeper. 'Nobody been by for the last ten minutes.'

'Did someone like that come into the gallery a little while ago?'

'No one that I recall. What did you say the bloke's name was?'

'Kipling,' I said.

'Don't know him.'
'Didn't you ever read *The Jungle Book*?'
'Sounds familiar. Tarzan stuff, wasn't it?'

I left the museum, and wandered about the streets for a long time, but I couldn't find Kipling anywhere. Was it the boom of London's traffic that I heard, or the boom of the Sutlej river racing through the valleys?

DEATH OF A FAMILIAR

When I learnt from a mutual acquaintance that my friend Sunil had been killed, I could not help feeling a little surprised, even shocked. Had Sunil killed somebody, it would not have surprised me in the least; he did not greatly value the lives of others. But for him to have been the victim was a sad reflection of his rapid decline.

He was twenty-one at the time of his death. Two friends of his had killed him, stabbing him several times with their knives. Their motive was said to have been revenge. Apparently, he had seduced their wives. They had invited him to a bar in Meerut, had plied him with country liquor, and had then accompanied him out into the cold air of a December night. It was drizzling a little. Near the bridge over the canal, one of his companions seized him from behind, while the other plunged a knife first into his stomach and then into his chest. When Sunil slumped forward, the other friend stabbed him in the back. A passing cyclist saw the little group, heard a cry and a groan, saw a blade flash in the light from his lamp. He pedalled furiously into town, burst into the kotwali and roused the sergeant on duty. Accompanied by two constables, they ran to the bridge but found the area deserted. It was only as the rising sun drew an open wound across the sky that they found Sunil's body on the canal bank, his head and shoulders on the sand, his legs in running water.

The barkeeper was able to describe Sunil's companions, and they were arrested that same morning from their homes. They had not found time to get rid of their blood-soaked clothes. As they were not known to me, I took very little interest in the proceedings against them; but I understand that they have appealed against their sentences of life imprisonment.

I was in Delhi at the time of the murder, and it was almost a year since I had last seen Sunil. We had both lived in Shahganj and had left the place for jobs; I to work in a newspaper office, he in a paper factory owned by an uncle. It had been hoped that he would in time acquire a sense of responsibility and some stability of character. But I had known Sunil for over two years, and in that time it had been made abundantly clear that he had not been born to fit in with the conventions. And as for character, his had the stability of a grasshopper. He was forever in search of new adventures and sensations, and this appetite of his for every novelty led him into some awkward situations.

He was a product of Partition, of the frontier provinces, of Anglo-Indian public schools, of films Indian and American, of medieval India, knights in armour, hippies, drugs, sex magazines and the subtropical Terai. Had he lived in the time of the Moguls, he might have governed a province with saturnine and spectacular success. Being born into the twentieth century, he was but a juvenile delinquent.

It must be said to his credit that he was a delinquent of charm and originality. I realized this when I first saw him, sitting on the wall of the football stadium, his long legs—looking even longer and thinner because of the tight trousers he wore—dangling over the wall, his chappals trailing in the dust of the road, while his white bush-shirt lay open, unbuttoned, showing his smooth brown chest. He had a smile on his long face, which, with its high cheekbones, gave his cheeks a cavernous look, an impression of unrequited hunger.

We were both watching the wrestling. Two practice bouts were in progress—one between two thin, undernourished boys, and the other between the master of the akhara and a bearded Sikh who drove trucks for a living. They struggled in the soft mud of the wrestling pit, their well-oiled bodies glistening in the sunlight that filtered through a massive banyan tree. I had been standing near the akhara for a few minutes when I became conscious of the young man's gaze. When I turned round to look at him, he smiled satanically.

'Are you a wrestler, too?' he asked.

'Do I look like one?' I countered.

'No, you look more like an athlete,' he said. 'I mean a long-distance runner. Very thin.'

'I'm a writer. Like long-distance runners most writers are very thin.'

'You're an Anglo-Indian, aren't you?'

'My family history is very complicated, otherwise I'd be delighted to give you all the details.'

'You could pass for a European, you know. You're quite fair. But you have an Indian accent.'

'An Indian accent is very similar to a Welsh accent,' I observed. 'I might pass for a Welsh, but not many people in India have met Welshmen!'

He chuckled at my answer, then stared at me speculatively. 'I say,' he said at length, as though an idea of great weight and importance had occurred to him. 'Do you have any magazines with pictures of dames?'

'Well, I may have some old *Playboys*. You can have them if you like.'

'Thanks,' he said, getting down from the wall. 'I'll come and fetch them. This wresting is boring, anyway.'

He slipped his hand into mine (a custom of no special significance), and began whistling snatches of Hindi film tunes and the latest American hits.

I was living at the time in a small flat above the town's main shopping centre. Below me there were shops, restaurants and a cinema. Behind the building lay a junkyard littered with the framework of vintage cars and broken-down tongas. I was paying thirty rupees a month for my two rooms, and sixty to the Punjabi restaurant where I took my meals. My earnings as a freelance writer were something like a hundred and fifty rupees a month, sufficient to enable me to make both ends meet, provided I remained in the backwater that was Shahganj.

Sunil (I had learnt his name during our walk from the stadium) made himself at home in my flat as soon as he entered it. He went through all my magazines, books and photographs with the thoroughness of an executor of a will. In India, it is customary for people to try and find out all there is to know about you, and Sunil went through the formalities with considerable thoroughness. While he spoke, his roving eyes made a mental inventory of all my belongings. These were few—a typewriter, a small radio and a cupboard full of books and clothes, besides the furniture that went with the flat. I had no valuables. Was he disappointed? I could not be sure. He wore good clothes and spoke fluent English, but good clothes and good English are no criteria for honesty. He was a little too glib to inspire confidence. Apparently, he was still at college. His father owned a cloth shop—a strict man who did not give his son much money to spend.

But Sunil was not seriously interested in money, as I was shortly to discover. He was interested in experience, and searched for it in various directions.

'You have a nice view,' he said, leaning over my balcony and looking up and down the street. 'You can see everyone on parade. Girls! They're becoming quite modern now. Short hair and small blouses. Tight salwars. Maxis, minis. Falsies. Do you like girls?'

'Well...' I began, but he did not really expect an answer to his question.

'"What are little girls made of?" That's an English poem, isn't it? "Sugar and spice and everything nice..." And I don't remember the rest.' He lowered his voice to a confidential undertone. 'Have you had any girls?'

'Well...'

'I had fun with a girl, you know, my cousin. She came to stay with us last summer. Then there's a girl in college who's stuck on me. But this is such a backward country. We can't be seen together in public and I can't invite her to my house. Can I bring her here some day?'

'Well, I don't know...' I hadn't lived in a small town like Shahganj for some time, and wasn't sure if morals had changed along with the fashions.

'Oh, not now,' he said. 'There's no hurry. I'll give you plenty of warning, don't worry.' He put an arm around my shoulders and looked at me with undisguised affection. 'We are going to be great friends, you and I.'

After that I began to receive almost daily visits from Sunil. His college classes got over at three in the afternoon, and though it was seldom that he attended them, he would stop at my place after putting in a brief appearance at the study hall. I could hardly blame him for neglecting his books, Shakespeare and Chaucer were prescribed for students who had but a rudimentary knowledge of modern English usage. Vast numbers of graduates were produced every year, and most of them became clerks or bus conductors or, perhaps, schoolteachers. But Sunil's father wanted the best for his son. And in Shahganj that meant as many degrees as possible.

Sunil would come stamping into my rooms, waking me from the siesta which had become a habit during summer afternoons. When he found that I did not relish being woken up, he would leave me to sleep while he took a bath under the tap. After making liberal use of my hair cream and aftershave lotion (he had just begun shaving, but used the lotion on his body), he would want to go to a movie theatre or a restaurant, and would sprinkle me with cold water so that I leapt off the bed.

One afternoon he felt more than usually ebullient, and poured a whole bucket of water over me, soaking the sheets and mattress. I retaliated by flinging the water jug at his head.

It missed him and shattered itself against the wall. Sunil then went berserk and started splashing water all over the room, while I threatened and shouted. When I tried restraining him by force, we rolled over on the ground, and I banged my head against the bedstead and almost lost consciousness. He was then full of contrition and massaged the lump on my head with hair cream and refused to borrow any money from me that day.

Sunil's 'borrowing' consisted of extracting a few rupees from my wallet, saying he needed the money for books or a tailor's bill or a shopkeeper who was threatening him with violence, and then spending it on something quite different. Before long I gave up asking him to return anything, just as I had given up asking him to stop seeing me.

Sunil was one of those people best loved from a distance. He was born with a special talent for trouble. I think it pleased his vanity when he was pursued by irate creditors, shopkeepers, brothers whose sisters he had insulted and husbands whose wives he had molested. My association with him did nothing to improve my own reputation in Shahganj.

My landlady, a protective motherly Punjabi widow said: 'Son, you are in bad company. Do you know that Sunil has already been expelled from one school for stealing and from another for sexual offences?'

'He's only a boy,' I said. 'And he's taking longer than most boys to grow up. He doesn't realize the seriousness of what he does. He will learn as he grows older.'

'If he grows older,' said my landlady darkly. 'Do you know that he nearly killed a man last year? When a fruit-seller who had been cheated threatened to report Sunil to the police, he threw a brick at the man's head. The poor man was in hospital for three weeks. If Sunil's father did not have political influence, the boy would be in jail now instead of climbing your stairs every afternoon.'

Once again I suggested to Sunil that he come to see me less often.

He looked hurt and offended.

'Don't you like me anymore?'

'I like you immensely. But I have work to do...'

'I know. You think I am a crook. Well, I am a crook.' He spoke with all the confidence of a young man who has never been hurt or disillusioned; he had romantic notions about swindlers and gangsters. 'I'll be a big crook one day, and people will be scared of me. But don't worry, old boy, you're my friend. I wouldn't harm you in any way. In fact, I'll protect you.'

'Thank you, but I don't require protection, I want to be left alone. I have work, and you are a worry and a distraction.'

'Well, I'm not going to leave you alone,' he said, assuming the posture of a spoilt child. 'Why should you be left alone? Who do you think you are? If we're friends now, it's your fault. I'm not going to buzz off just to suit your convenience.'

'Come less often, that's all.'

'I'll come more often, you old snob! I know you're thinking of your reputation—as if you had any. Well, you don't have to worry, *mon ami*—as they say in Hollywood. I'll be very discreet, Daddyji!'

Whenever I complained or became querulous, Sunil would call me daddy or uncle or sometimes mum, and make me feel more ridiculous. If he was in a good mood, he would use the

Hindi word chacha (uncle). All it did was to make me feel much older than my twenty-five years.

Sunil turned up one afternoon with blood streaming from his nose and from a gash across his forehead. He sat down at the foot of the bed and began dabbing his face with the bedsheet.

'What have you done to yourself?' I asked in some alarm.

'Some fellows beat me up. There were three of them. They followed me on their cycles.'

'Who were they?' I asked, looking for iodine on the dressing table.

'Just some fellows...'

'They must have had a reason.'

'Well, a sister of one of them had been talking to me.'

'Well, that isn't a reason even in Shahganj. You must have said or done something to offend her.'

'No, she likes me,' he said, wincing as I dabbed iodine on his forehead. 'We went to the guava orchard near my uncle's farm.'

'She went out there alone with you?'

'Sure. I took her on my bike. They must have followed us. Anyway, we weren't doing much except kissing and fooling around. But some people seem to think that's worse than...'

Both he and the other boys of Shahganj had grown up to look upon girls as strange, exotic animals, who must be seized at the first opportunity. Experimenting with sex was like playing a surreptitious game of marbles.

Sunil produced a clasp knife from his pocket, opened it and held the blade against the flat of his hand.

'Don't worry, Uncle. I can look after myself. The next fellow who tries to interfere with me will get this in his guts.'

'Don't be silly,' I said. 'You will go to prison for ten years. Listen, I'm going up to Simla for a couple of weeks, just for a change. Why don't you come with me? It will be a pleasant change from Shahganj, and in the meantime all this fuss will die down.'

It was one of those invitations which I make so readily and instantly regret. As soon as I had made the suggestion, I realized that Sunil in Simla might be even more of a problem than Sunil in Shahganj. But it was too late for me to back out.

'Simla! Why not? The college is closing for the summer holidays, and my father won't mind my going with you. He believes you're the only respectable friend I've got. Boy! We'll have a good time in Simla.'

'You'll have to behave yourself there, if you want to come with me. No girls, Sunil.'

'No girls, Sir. I'll be very good, Chachaji. Please take me to Simla.'

'I think two hundred rupees should be enough for a fortnight for both of us,' I said.

'Oh, too much,' said Sunil modestly.

'And a week later we were actually in Simla, putting up at a moderately priced, middle-class hotel.

Our first few days in the hill station were pleasant enough. We went for long walks, tired ourselves out and acquired enormous appetites. Sunil, in the hills for the first time in his life, declared that they were wonderful, and thanked me a score of times for bringing him along. He took a genuine interest in exploring remote valleys, forests and waterfalls, and seemed to be losing some of his self-centredness. I believe that mountains do affect one's personality, if one can remain among them long enough; and if Sunil had grown up in the hills instead of a refugee township, I have no doubt he would have been a completely different person.

There was one small waterfall I rather liked. It was down a ravine, in a rather inaccessible spot, where very few people ever went. The water fell about thirty feet into a small pool. We bathed here on two occasions, and Sunil quite forgot the attractions of the town. And we would have visited the spot again had I not slipped and sprained my ankle. This accident confined me to the hotel balcony for several days, and I was afraid that Sunil, for want of companionship, would go in search of more mundane distractions. But though he went out often enough, he came back dusty and sunburnt; and the fact that he asked me for very little money was evidence enough of his fondness for the outdoors. Striding through forests of oak and pine, with all the world stretched out far below, was no doubt a new and exhilarating experience for him. But how long would it be before the spell was broken?

'Don't you need any money?' I asked him uneasily, on the third day of his Thoreau-like activities.

'What for, Uncle? Fresh air costs nothing. And besides, I don't owe money to anyone in Simla. We haven't been here long enough.'

'Then perhaps we should be going,' I said.

'Shahganj is a miserable little dump.'

'I know, but it's your home. And for the time being, it's mine.'

'Listen, Uncle,' he said, after a moment of reflection, 'yesterday, on one of my walks, I met a schoolteacher. She's over thirty, so don't get nervous. She doesn't have any brothers or relatives who will come chasing after me. And she's much fairer than you, Uncle. Is it all right if I'm friendly with her?'

'I suppose so,' I said uncertainly. Schoolteachers can usually take care of themselves (if they want to), besides, an older woman might have a sobering influence on Sunil.

He brought her over to see me that same evening, and seemed quite proud of his new acquisition. She was indeed fair, perhaps insipidly so, with blonde hair and light blue eyes. She had a young face and a healthy body, but her voice was peculiarly toneless and flat, giving an impression of boredom, of lassitude. I wondered what she found attractive in Sunil apart from his obvious animal charm. They had hardly anything in common, but perhaps the absence of similar interests was an attraction in itself. In six or seven years of teaching, Maureen must have been tired of the usual scholastic types. Sunil was refreshingly free from all classroom associations.

Maureen let her hair down at the first opportunity. She switched on the bedroom radio and found Ceylon. Soon she was teaching Sunil to dance. This was amusing, because Sunil, with his long legs, had great difficulty in taking small steps; nor could Maureen cope with his great strides. But he was very earnest about it all, and inserting an unlit cigarette between his lips, did his best to move rhythmically around the bedroom. I think he was convinced that by learning to dance he would reach the high watermark of Western culture. Maureen stood for all that was remote and romantic, and for all the films that he had seen, to conquer her would, for Sunil, be a voyage of discovery and not a mere gratification of his senses. And for

Maureen, this new unconventional friendship must have been a refreshing diversion from the dreariness of her school routine. She was old enough to realize that it was only a diversion. The intensity of emotional attachments had faded with her early youth and love could wound her heart no more. But for Sunil, it was only the beginning of something that stirred him deeply, moved him inexorably towards manhood.

It was unfortunate that I did not then notice this subtle change in my friend. I had known him only as a shallow creature, and was certain that this new infatuation would disappear as soon as the novelty of it wore off. As Maureen had no encumbrances, no relations that she would speak of, I saw no harm in encouraging the friendship and seeing how it would develop.

'I think we'd better have something to drink,' I said, and ringing the bell for the room bearer, ordered several bottles of beer.

Sunil gave me an odd, whimsical look. I had never before encouraged him to drink. But he did not hesitate to open the bottles, and, before long, Maureen and he were drinking from the same glass.

'Let's make love,' said Sunil, putting his arm around Maureen's shoulders and gazing adoringly into her dreamy blue eyes.

They seemed unconcerned by my presence; but I was embarrassed, and, getting up, said I would be going for a walk.

'Enjoy yourself,' said Sunil, winking at me over Maureen's shoulder.

'You ought to get yourself a girlfriend,' said the young woman in a conciliatory tone.

'True,' I said, and moved guiltily out of the room I was paying for.

Our stay in Simla lasted several days longer than we had planned. I saw little of Sunil and Maureen during this time. As Sunil had no desire to return to Shahganj any earlier than was absolutely necessary, he avoided me during the day but I managed to stay awake late enough one night to confront him when he crept quietly into the room.

'Dear friend and familiar,' I said. 'I hate to spoil your beautiful romance, but I have absolutely no money left, and unless you have resources of your own—or if Maureen can support you—I suggest that you accompany me back to Shahganj the day after tomorrow.'

'How mean you are, Chachaji. This is something serious. I mean Maureen and me. Do you think we should get married?'

'No.'

'But why not?'

'Because she cannot support you on a teacher's salary. And she probably isn't interested in a permanent relationship—like ours.'

'Very funny. And you think I'd let my wife slave for me?'

'I do. And besides...'

'And besides,' he interrupted, grinning, 'she's old enough to be my mother.'

'Are you really in love with her?' I asked him. 'I've never known you to be serious about anything.'

'Honestly, Uncle.'

'And what about her?'

'Oh, she loves me terribly, really she does. She's ready to come down with us if it's possible. Only I've told her that I'll first have to break the news to my father, otherwise he might kick me out of the house.'

'Well, then,' I said shrewdly, 'the sooner we return to Shahganj and get your father's blessings, the sooner you and Maureen can get married, if that's what both of you really want.'

Early next morning Sunil disappeared, and I knew he would be gone all day. My foot was better, and I decided to take a walk on my own to the waterfall I had liked so much. It was almost noon when I reached the spot and began descending the steep path to the ravine. The stream was hidden by dense foliage, giant ferns and dahlias, but the water made a tremendous noise as it tumbled over the rocks. When I reached a sharp promontory, I was able to look down on the pool. Two people were lying on the grass.

I did not recognize them at first. They looked very beautiful together, and I had not expected Sunil and Maureen to look so beautiful. Sunil, on whom no surplus flesh had as yet gathered, possessed all the sinuous grace and power of a young god; and the woman, her white flesh pressed against young grass, reminded me of a painting by Titian that I had seen in a gallery in Florence. Her full, mature body was touched with a tranquil intoxication, her breasts rose and fell slowly, and waves of muscle merged into the shadows of her broad thighs. It was as though I had stumbled into another age, and had found two lovers in a forest glade. Only a fool would have wished to disturb them. Sunil had for once in his life risen above mediocrity, and I hurried away before the magic was lost.

The human voice often shatters the beauty of the most tender passions; and when we left Simla the next day, and Maureen and Sunil used all the stock cliches to express their love, I was a little disappointed. But the poetry of life was in their bodies, not in their tongues.

Back in Shahganj, Sunil actually plucked up the courage to speak to his father. This, to me, was a sign that he took the affair very seriously, for he seldom approached his father for anything. But all the sympathy that he received was a box on the ears. I received a curt note suggesting that I was having a corrupting influence on the boy and that I should stop seeing him. There was little I could do in the matter, because it had always been Sunil who had insisted on seeing me.

He continued to visit me, bring me Maureen's letters (strange, how lovers cannot bear that the world should not know their love), and his own to her, so that I could correct his English!

It was at about this time that Sunil began speaking to me about his uncle's paper factory and the possibility of working in it. Once he was getting a salary, he pointed out, Maureen would be able to leave her job and join him.

Unfortunately, Sunil's decision to join the paper factory took months to crystallize into a definite course of action, and in the meantime he was finding a panacea for lovesickness in rum and sometimes cheap country spirit. The money that he now borrowed was used not to pay his debts, or to incur new ones, but to drink himself silly. I regretted having been the first person to have offered him a drink. I should have known that Sunil was a person who could do nothing in moderation.

He pestered me less often now, but the purpose of his occasional visits became all too obvious. I was having a little success, and thoughtlessly gave Sunil the few rupees he usually demanded. At the same time I was beginning to find other friends, and I no longer found myself worrying about Sunil, as I had so often done in the past. Perhaps this was treachery on my part...

When finally I decided to leave Shahganj for Delhi, I went in search of Sunil to say goodbye. I found him in a small bar, alone at a table with a bottle of rum. Though barely twenty, he no longer looked a boy. He was a completely different person from the handsome, cocksure youth I had met at the wrestling pit a year previously. His cheeks were hollow and he had not shaved for days. I knew that when I first met him he had been without scruples, a shallow youth, the product of many circumstances. He was no longer so shallow and he had stumbled upon love, but his character was too weak to sustain the weight of disillusionment. Perhaps I should have left him severely alone from the beginning. Before me sat a ruin, and I had helped to undermine the foundation. None of us can really avoid seeing the outcome of our smallest actions...

'I'm off to Delhi, Sunil.'

He did not look up from the table.

'Have a good time,' he said.

'Have you heard from Maureen?' I asked, certain that he had not.

He nodded, but for once did not offer to show me the letter.

'What's wrong?' I asked.

'Oh, nothing,' he said, looking up and forcing a smile. 'These dames are all the same, Uncle. We shouldn't take them too seriously, you know.'

'Why, what has she done, got married to someone else?'

'Yes,' he said scornfully. 'To a bloody teacher.'

'Well, she wasn't young,' I said. 'She couldn't wait for you forever, I suppose.'

'She could if she had really loved me. But there's no such thing as love, is there, Uncle?'

I made no reply. Had he really broken his heart over a woman? Were there, within him, unsuspected depths of feeling and passion? You find love when you least expect to and lose it when you are sure that it is in your grasp.

'You're a lucky beggar,' he said. 'You're a philosopher. You find a reason for every stupid thing and so you are able to ignore all stupidity.'

I laughed. 'You're becoming a philosopher yourself. But don't think too hard, Sunil, you might find it painful.'

'Not I, Chachaji,' he said, emptying his glass. 'I'm not going to think. I'm going to work in a paper factory. I shall become respectable. What an adventure that will be!'

And that was the last time I saw Sunil.

He did not become respectable. He was still searching like a great discoverer for something new, someone different, when he met his pitiful end in the cold rain of a December night.

Though murder cases usually get reported in the papers, Sunil was a person of such little importance that his violent end was not considered newsworthy. It went unnoticed, and Maureen could not have known about it. The case has already been forgotten, for in the great human mass that is India, hundreds of people disappear every day and are never heard of again. Sunil will be quickly forgotten by all except those to whom he owed money.

A CASE FOR INSPECTOR LAL

I met Inspector Keemat Lal about two years ago, while I was living in the hot, dusty town of Shahpur in the plains of northern India.

Keemat Lal had charge of the local police station. He was a heavily built man, slow and rather ponderous, and inclined to be lazy; but, like most lazy people, he was intelligent. He was also a failure. He had remained an Inspector for a number of years, and had given up all hopes of a further promotion. His luck was against him, he said. He should never have been a policeman. He had been born under the sign of Capricorn and should really have gone into the restaurant business; but now it was too late to do anything about it.

The Inspector and I had little in common. He was nearing forty, and I was twenty-five. But both of us spoke English, and in Shahpur there were very few people who did. In addition, we were both fond of beer. There were no places of entertainment in Shahpur. The searing heat, the dust that came whirling up from the east, the mosquitoes (almost as numerous as the flies), and the general monotony gave one a thirst for something more substantial than stale lemonade.

My house was on the outskirts of the town, where we were often not disturbed. On two or three evenings in the week, just as the sun was going down and making it possible for one to emerge from the khas-cooled confines of a dark, high-ceilinged bedroom, Inspector Keemat Lal would appear on the verandah steps, mopping the sweat from his face with a small towel, which he used instead of a handkerchief. My only servant, excited at the prospect of serving an inspector of police, would hurry out with glasses, a bucket of ice and several bottles of the best Indian beer.

One evening, after we had overtaken our fourth bottle, I said, 'You must have had some interesting cases in your career, Inspector.'

'Most of them were rather dull,' he said. 'At least the successful ones were. The sensational cases usually went unsolved—otherwise I might have been a superintendent by now. I suppose you are talking of murder cases. Do you remember the shooting of the Minister of the Interior? I was on that one, but it was a political murder and we never solved it.'

'Tell me about a case you solved,' I said. 'An interesting one.' When I saw him looking uncomfortable, I added, 'You don't have to worry, Inspector. I'm a very discreet person, in spite of all the beer I consume.'

'But how can you be discreet? You are a writer.'

I protested: 'Writers are usually very discreet. They always change the names of people and places.'

He gave me one of his rare smiles. 'And how would you describe me, if you were to put me into a story?'

'Oh, I'd leave you as you are. No one would believe in you, anyway.'

He laughed indulgently and poured out more beer. 'I suppose I can change names, too... I will tell you a very interesting case. The victim was an unusual person, and so was the killer. But you must promise not to write this story.'

'I promise,' I lied.

'Do you know Panauli?'

'In the hills? Yes, I have been there once or twice.'

'Good, then you will follow me without my having to be too descriptive. This happened about three years ago, shortly after I had been stationed at Panauli. Nothing much ever happened there. There were a few cases of theft and cheating, and an occasional fight during the summer. A murder took place about once every ten years. It was, therefore, quite an event when the Rani of— was found dead in her sitting-room, her head split open by an axe. I knew that I would have to solve the case if I wanted to stay in Panauli.

'The trouble was, anyone could have killed the Rani, and there were some who made no secret of their satisfaction that she was dead. She had been an unpopular woman. Her husband was dead, her children were scattered, and her money—for she had never been a very wealthy Rani—had been dwindling away. She lived alone in an old house on the outskirts of the town, ruling the locality with the stern authority of a matriarch. She had a servant, and he was the man who found the body and came to the police, dithering and tongue-tied. I arrested him at once, of course. I knew he was probably innocent, but a basic rule is to grab the first man on the scene of the crime, especially if he happens to be a servant. But we let him go after a beating. There was nothing much he could tell us, and he had a sound alibi.

'The axe with which the Rani had been killed must have been a small woodcutter's axe—so we deduced from the wound. We couldn't find the weapon. It might have been used by a man or a woman, and there were several of both sexes who had a grudge against the Rani. There were bazaar rumours that she had been supplementing her income by trafficking in young women: she had the necessary connections. There were also rumours that she possessed vast wealth, and that it was stored away in her godowns. We did not find any treasure. There were so many rumours darting about like battered shuttlecocks that I decided to stop wasting my time in trying to follow them up. Instead I restricted my enquiries to those people who had been close to the Rani—either in their personal relationships or in actual physical proximity.

'To begin with, there was Mr Kapur, a wealthy businessman from Bombay who had a house in Panauli. He was supposed to be an old admirer of the Rani's. I discovered that he had occasionally lent her money, and that, in spite of his professed friendship for her, he had charged a high rate of interest.

'Then there were her immediate neighbours—an American missionary and his wife, who had been trying to convert the Rani to Christianity; an English spinster of seventy who made no secret of the fact that she and the Rani had hated each other with great enthusiasm; a local councillor and his family, who did not get on well with their aristocratic neighbour; and a tailor, who kept his shop close by. None of these people had any powerful motive for killing the Rani—or none that I could discover. But the tailor's daughter interested me.

'Her name was Kusum. She was twelve or thirteen years old—a thin dark girl, with lovely black eyes and a swift, disarming smile. While I was making my routine enquiries in the vicinity of the Rani's house, I noticed that the girl always tried to avoid me. When I questioned her about the Rani, and about her own movements on the day of the crime, she pretended to be very vague and stupid.

'But I could see she was not stupid, and I became convinced that she knew something unusual about the Rani. She might even know something about the murder. She could have been protecting someone, and was afraid to tell me what she knew. Often, when I spoke to her of the violence of the Rani's death, I saw fear in her eyes. I began to think the girl's life might be in danger, and I had a close watch kept on her. I liked her. I liked her youth and freshness and the innocence and wonder in her eyes. I spoke to her whenever I could, kindly and paternally, and though I knew she rather liked me and found me amusing—the ups and downs of Panauli always left me panting for breath—and though I could see that she *wanted* to tell me something, she always held back at the last moment.

'Then, one afternoon while I was in the Rani's house going through her effects, I saw something glistening in a narrow crack near the doorstep. I would not have noticed it if the sun had not been pouring through the window, glinting off the little object. I stooped and picked up a piece of glass. It was part of a broken bangle.

'I turned the fragment over in my hand. There was something familiar about its colour and design. Didn't Kusum wear similar glass bangles? I went to look for the girl but she was not at her father's shop. I was told that she had gone down the hill, to gather firewood.

'I decided to take the narrow path down the hill. It went round some rocks and cactus, and then disappeared into a forest of oak trees. I found Kusum sitting at the edge of the forest, a bundle of twigs beside her.

"You are always wandering about alone," I said. "Don't you feel afraid?"

"It is safer when I am alone," she replied. "Nobody comes here."

'I glanced quickly at the bangles on her wrist, and noticed that their colour matched that of the broken piece. I held out the bit of broken glass and said, "I found it in the Rani's house. It must have fallen…"

'She did not wait for me to finish what I was saying. With a look of terror, she sprang up from the grass and fled into the forest.

'I was completely taken aback. I had not expected such a reaction. Of what significance was the broken bangle? I hurried after the girl, slipping on the smooth pine needles that covered the slopes. I was searching amongst the trees when I heard someone sobbing behind me. When I turned round, I saw the girl standing on a boulder, facing me with an axe in her hands.

'When Kusum saw me staring at her, she raised the axe and rushed down the slope towards me.

'I was too bewildered to be able to do anything but stare with open mouth as she rushed at me with the axe. The impetus of her run would have brought her right up against me, and the axe, coming down, would probably have crushed my skull, thick though it is. But while she was still six feet from me, the axe flew out of her hands. It sprang into the air as though it had a life of its own and came curving towards me.

'In spite of my weight, I moved swiftly aside. The axe grazed my shoulder and sank into the soft bark of the tree behind me. And Kusum dropped at my feet, weeping hysterically.

Inspector Keemat Lal paused in order to replenish his glass. He took a long pull at the beer, and the froth glistened on his moustache.

'And then what happened?' I prompted him.

'Perhaps it could only have happened in India—and to a person like me,' he said. 'This sudden compassion for the person you are supposed to destroy. Instead of being furious and outraged, instead of seizing the girl and marching her off to the police station, I stroked her head and said silly comforting things.'

'And she told you that she had killed the Rani?'

'She told me how the Rani had called her to her house and given her tea and sweets. Mr Kapur had been there. After some time he began stroking Kusum's arms and squeezing her knees. She had drawn away, but Kapur kept pawing her. The Rani was telling Kusum not to be afraid, that no harm would come to her. Kusum slipped away from the man and made a rush for the door. The Rani caught her by the shoulders and pushed her back into the room. The Rani was getting angry. Kusum saw the axe lying in a corner of the room. She seized it, raised it above her head and threatened Kapur. The man realized that he had gone too far, and, valuing his neck, backed away. But the Rani, in a great rage, sprang at the girl. And Kusum, in desperation and panic, brought the axe down across the Rani's head.'

'The Rani fell to the ground. Without waiting to see what Kapur might do, Kusum fled from the house. Her bangle must have broken when she stumbled against the door. She ran into the forest and, after concealing the axe amongst some tall ferns, lay weeping on the grass until it grew dark. But such was her nature, and such the resilience of youth, that she recovered sufficiently to be able to return home looking her normal self. And during the following days she managed to remain silent about the whole business.'

'What did you do about it?' I asked.

Keemat Lal looked me straight in my beery eye.

'Nothing,' he said. 'I did absolutely nothing. I couldn't have the girl put away in a remand home. It would have crushed her spirit.'

'And what about Kapur?'

'Oh, he had his own reasons for remaining quiet, as you may guess. No, the case was closed—or perhaps I should say the file was put in my pending tray. My promotion, too, went into the pending tray.'

'It didn't turn out very well for you,' I said.

'No. Here I am in Shahpur, and still an Inspector. But, tell me, what would you have done if you had been in my place?'

I considered his question carefully for a moment or two, then said, 'I suppose it would have depended on how much sympathy the girl evoked in me. She had killed in innocence...'

'Then you would have put your personal feelings above your duty to uphold the law?'

'Yes. But I would not have made a very good policeman.'

'Exactly.'

'Still, it's a pity that Kapur got off so easily.'

'There was no alternative if I was to let the girl go. But he didn't get off altogether. He found himself in trouble later for swindling some manufacturing concern, and went to jail for a couple of years.'

'And the girl—did you see her again?'

'Well, before I was transferred from Panauli, I saw her occasionally on the road. She was usually on her way to school. She would greet me with joined palms, and call me Uncle.'

The beer bottles were all empty, and Inspector Keemat Lal got up to leave. His final words to me were, 'I should never have been a policeman.'

THE BENT-DOUBLE BEGGAR

The person I encounter most often on the road is old Ganpat, the bent-double beggar. Every morning he hobbles up and down the road below my rooms, biding his time, and suddenly manifesting himself in front of unwary passers-by or shoppers. It is difficult to resist Ganpat because, though bent double, he is very dignified. He has a long, white beard and commanding eyes. His voice is powerful and carries well, which is probably why people say he was once an actor.

People say many things about him. One rumour has it that he was once a well-to-do lawyer with a European wife: a paralytic stroke put an end to his career, and his wife finally left him. I have also been told that he is a CID man in disguise—a rumour that might well have been started by Ganpat himself.

I was curious to know the true story of his life, for I was convinced that he was not a beggar by choice; he had little in common with other members of his profession. His English was good, and he could recite passages from Shakespeare; his Hindi was excellent. He never made a direct request for money, but would enter into conversation with you, and remark on the weather or the innate meanness of the human race, until you slipped him a coin.

'Look, Ganpat,' I said one day, 'I've heard a lot of stories about you, and I don't know which is true. How did you become a beggar? How did you get your crooked back?'

'That's a very long story,' he said, flattered by my interest in him. 'I don't know if you will believe it. Besides, it is not to everyone that I would speak freely.'

He had served his purpose in whetting my appetite. I said, 'It will be worth a rupee if you tell me your story.'

He stroked his beard, considering my offer.

'Very well,' he said, squatting down on his haunches, while I pulled myself up on a low wall. 'But it happened more than twenty years ago, and you cannot expect me to remember the details very clearly...'

'In those days,' said Ganpat, 'I was a healthy young man, with a wife and baby daughter. I owned a few acres of land, and, though we were not rich, we were not very poor. When I took my produce to the market, five miles away, I harnessed the bullocks and drove down the dusty village road, sometimes returning home late at night.

'Every night I passed a peepul tree, which was said to be haunted, I had never met the ghost, and did not really believe in him, but his name, I was told, was Bippin, and long ago he had been hanged from the peepul tree by a gang of dacoits. Since then this ghost had lived in the tree, and was in the habit of pouncing upon any person who resembled a dacoit and beating him severely. I suppose I must have looked a little guilty after a particularly successful business deal, because one night Bippin decided to pounce on me. He leapt out of the tree and stood in the middle of the road, bringing my bullocks to a halt.

"'You, there,' he shouted. "Get off your cart, I am going to thrash you and then string you up from this tree!"

'I was of course considerably alarmed, but decided to put on a bold front.' "I have no intention of getting off my cart. If you like, you can climb up yourself!"

"'Spoken like a man,' said Bippin, and he jumped up beside me. "But tell me one good reason for not stringing you up."

"'I am not a dacoit,' I replied.

"'But you look as though you could be one. That is the same thing."

"'I am a poor man, with a wife and child to support."

"'You have no business being poor,' said Bippin angrily.

"'Well, make me rich if you can."

"'Do you not believe I can? Do you defy me to make you rich?"

"'Certainly,' I said. "I defy you to make me rich."

"'Then drive on,' cried Bippin. "I am coming home with you."

'And I drove on to the village with Bippin sitting beside me.

"'I have so arranged it,' he said, "that no one will be able to see me. And another thing. I must sleep beside you every night, and no one must know of it. Should you tell anyone about my presence, I will not hesitate to strangle you!"

"'You needn't worry,' I said. "I won't tell any one."

"'Good. I look forward to living with you. It was getting lonely in that peepul tree."

'And so Bippin came to live with me, and he slept beside me every night; and we got on very well together. He kept his promise, and money began to pour in from every conceivable source, until I was in a position to buy more land and cattle. Nobody knew of our association, though naturally my friends and relatives wondered where all the money was coming from. At the same time, my wife was rather upset at my unwillingness to sleep beside her at night. I could not very well put her in the same bed with a ghost, and Bippin was most particular about sleeping near me. At first I told my wife that I wasn't well, and that I would sleep on the verandah. Then I told her that there was someone after our cows, and that I would have to keep an eye on them at night. Bippin and I slept in the cow-house.

'My wife would often spy on me at night, suspecting infidelity; but she always found me lying alone amongst the cows. Unable to understand my strange behaviour, she mentioned it to her family; and next day my in-laws arrived on our doorstep, demanding an explanation.

'At the same time my own relatives were insisting that I give them some explanation for my own rapidly increasing fortune. Uncles and aunts and distant cousins descended on me from all parts of the country, wanting to know where the money was coming from, and hoping to have some share of it.

'"Do you all want me to die?" I said, losing my patience with them. "I am under an oath of silence. If I tell you the source of my wealth, I will be signing my own death warrant."

'But they laughed at me, taking this for a lame excuse; they suspected I was trying to keep my fortune to myself. My wife's relatives suspected that I had found another woman. Finally, I became so exasperated with their questions and demands that in a moment of weakness I blurted out the truth.

'They didn't believe the truth (who does?), but it gave them something to think about and talk about, and they left me in peace for a few days.

'But that same night Bippin did not come to sleep beside me. I was left alone with the cows. When he did not come the following night, I was afraid that he would throttle me while I slept. I was almost certain that my good fortune had come to an end, and I went back to sleeping in my own house.

'The next time I was driving back to the village from the market, Bippin leapt out of the peepul tree.

'"False friend," he cried, halting the bullocks. "I gave you everything you wanted, and still you betrayed me!"

'"I'm very sorry," I said. "But as a ghost you wouldn't understand what a man's relatives can be like. You can of course hang me from the peepul tree, if you wish."

"No, I cannot kill you," he said. "We have been friends for too long. But I must punish you all the same."

'Picking up a stout stick, he struck me three times across the back, until I was bent double.

'After that,' concluded Ganpat, 'I could never straighten myself up again, and for twenty years I have been a crooked man. My wife left me and went back to her family, and I could no longer work in the fields. I left my village and wandered from one city to another, begging for a living. That is how I came here. People in this town seem to be more generous than elsewhere.'

He looked at me with his most appealing smile, waiting for the promised rupee.

'You can't expect me to believe that story,' I said. 'But for your powers of invention you deserve a rupee.'

'No, no,' said Ganpat, hacking away and affecting indignation. 'If you don't believe me, keep the rupee!'

Finally, he permitted me to force the note into his hand, and then he went hobbling away to the bazaar. I was almost certain he had been telling me a very tall story. But you can never really be sure. Perhaps it was true about Bippin. And it was clever to give him the rupee, just in case he was, after all, a CID man.

Some Teachings of the Bent-Double Beggar

'A woman can become jealous of anyone, anything,' maintained Ganpat. 'Even of a ghost.'

◆

'You must love everyone,' said the bent-double beggar.

'Even my enemies?' I asked.

'It is difficult to love your enemies. Much simpler not to have enemies.'

◆

Observed a naked ascetic 'meditating' beneath a peepul tree.

'He is superior to us,' I said. 'He has conquered all desires. We cannot be like that, Ganpat.'

'You think so? Well, let's see...' And approaching the ascetic, he said, 'Babaji, can you teach us to meditate as you do?'

'Yes, I will teach you,' said the other readily. 'It will cost only fifty rupees a lesson.'

'You see?' said Ganpat, turning to me. 'There is indeed some purpose—even desire—in his meditation. I must remember to charge a fee the next time you ask me for advice.'

◆

Ganpat the bent-double beggar used to say that if all the troubles in the world could be laid down in one big heap, and everyone was allowed to choose one trouble, we will end up picking up our old trouble again.

◆

He saw in the commonplace what others did not see. A snake. He taught me to see not only the snake, but the path taken by the snake, the beauty of its movements; both the nature of the snake and the nature of the path. He taught me to be that snake, even if it was only for the duration of its passing.

◆

'I asked you to my party, but you did not come,' I complained.
'You asked me, that is the important thing. What does it matter if I did not come? You wanted me there, amongst your rich friends. That knowledge gave me all the refreshment I needed.'
In this life all our desires are fulfilled, on the condition that they do not bring the happiness we expected from them.

◆

It is no use getting upset about delays in India; they come with unfailing punctuality.

◆

His favourite proverb: if you must eat dung, eat elephant's dung.

◆

One can forgive ignorance in a man who has had little or no education; but ignorance in a man who has been to college is unforgivable. Yet it is quite common.

For democracy to succeed, the first requirement is that the majority of people should be honest.

◆

Nietzsche was wrong; it isn't action but pleasure that binds us to existence.

It is difficult to be miserable all the time. Human nature won't permit it. Even when we are burning or burying out dead, we are thinking of what we will eat or drink later in the day.

◆

Chance, gives, and takes away, and gives again.

◆

I travelled a lot once (said Ganpat), but you can go on doing that and not get anywhere. Wherever you go or whatever you do, *most* of your life will have to happen in your mind. And there's no escape from that little room!

THE STORY OF MADHU

I met little Madhu several years ago, when I lived alone in an obscure town near the Himalayan foothills. I was in my late twenties then, and my outlook on life was still quite romantic; the cynicism that was to come with the thirties had not yet set in.

I preferred the solitude of the small district town to the kind of social life I might have found in the cities; and in my books, my writing and the surrounding hills, there was enough for my pleasure and occupation.

On summer mornings I would often sit beneath an old mango tree, with a notebook or a sketch pad on my knees. The house which I had rented (for a very nominal sum) stood on the outskirts of the town; and a large tank and a few poor houses could be seen from the garden wall. A narrow public pathway passed under the low wall.

One morning, while I sat beneath the mango tree, I saw a young girl of about nine, wearing torn clothes, darting about on the pathway and along the high banks of the tank.

Sometimes she stopped to look at me; and, when I showed that I noticed her, she felt encouraged and gave me a shy, fleeting smile. The next day I discovered her leaning over the garden wall, following my actions as I paced up and down on the grass.

In a few days an acquaintance had been formed. I began to take the girl's presence for granted, and even to look for her; and she, in turn, would linger about on the pathway until she saw me come out of the house.

One day, as she passed the gate, I called her to me. 'What is your name?' I asked. 'And where do you live?'

'Madhu,' she said, brushing back her long untidy black hair and smiling at me from large black eyes. She pointed across the road: 'I live with my grandmother.'

'Is she very old?' I asked.

Madhu nodded confidingly and whispered: 'A hundred years…'

'We will never be that old,' I said. She was very slight and frail, like a flower growing in a rock, vulnerable to wind and rain.

I discovered later that the old lady was not her grandmother but a childless woman who had found the baby girl on the banks of the tank. Madhu's real parentage was unknown; but the wizened old woman had, out of compassion, brought up the child as her own.

My gate once entered, Madhu included the garden in her circle of activities. She was there every morning, chasing butterflies, stalking squirrels and mynahs, her voice brimming with laughter, her slight figure flitting about between the trees.

Sometimes, but not often, I gave her a toy or a new dress; and one day she put aside her shyness and brought me a present of a nosegay, made up of marigolds and wild blue cotton flowers.

'For you,' she said, and put the flowers in my lap.

'They are very beautiful,' I said, picking out the brightest marigold and putting it in her hair. 'But they are not as beautiful as you.'

Over a year passed before I began to take more than a mildly patronizing interest in Madhu.

It occurred to me after some time that she should be taught to read and write, and I asked a local teacher to give her lessons in the garden for an hour every day. She clapped her hands with pleasure at the prospect of what was to be for her a fascinating new game.

In a few weeks Madhu was surprising us with her capacity for absorbing knowledge. She always came to me to repeat the lessons of the day, and pestered me with questions on a variety of subjects. How big was the world? And were the stars really like our world? Or were they the sons and daughters of the sun and the moon?

My interest in Madhu deepened, and my life, so empty till then, became imbued with a new purpose. As she sat on the grass beside me, reading aloud, or listening to me with a look of complete trust and belief, all the love that had been lying dormant in me during my years of self-exile surfaced in a sudden surge of tenderness.

Three years glided away imperceptibly, and at the age of thirteen Madhu was on the verge of blossoming into a woman. I began to feel a certain responsibility towards her.

It was dangerous, I knew, to allow a child so pretty to live almost alone and unprotected, and to run unrestrained about the grounds. And in a censorious society she would be made to suffer if she spent too much time in my company.

She could see no need for any separation; but I decided to send her to a mission school in the next district, where I could visit her from time to time.

'But why?' said Madhu. 'I can learn more from you, and from the teacher who comes. I am so happy here.'

'You will meet other girls and make many friends,' I told her. 'I will come to see you. And, when you come home, we will be even happier. It is good that you should go.'

It was the middle of June, a hot and oppressive month in the Siwaliks. Madhu had expressed her readiness to go to school, and when, one evening, I did not see her as usual in the garden, I thought nothing of it; but the next day I was informed that she had fever and could not leave the house.

Illness was something Madhu had not known before, and for this reason I felt afraid. I hurried down the path which led to the old woman's cottage. It seemed strange that I had never once entered it during my long friendship with Madhu.

It was a humble mud hut, the ceiling just high enough to enable me to stand upright, the room dark but clean. Madhu was lying on a string cot exhausted by fever, her eyes closed, her long hair unkempt, one small hand hanging over the side.

It struck me then how little, during all this time, I had thought of her physical comforts. There was no chair; I knelt down, and took her hand in mine. I knew, from the fierce heat of her body, that she was seriously ill.

She recognized my touch, and a smile passed across her face before she opened her eyes. She held on to my hand, then laid it across her cheek.

I looked round the little room in which she had grown up. It had scarcely an article of furniture apart from two string cots, on one of which the old woman sat and watched us, her white, wizened head nodding like a puppet's.

In a corner lay Madhu's little treasures. I recognized among them the presents which during the past four years I had given her. She had kept everything. On her dark arm she still wore a small piece of ribbon which I had playfully tied there about a year ago. She had given her heart, even before she was conscious of possessing one, to a stranger unworthy of the gift.

As the evening drew on, a gust of wind blew open the door of the dark room, and a gleam of sunshine streamed in, lighting up a portion of the wall. It was the time when every evening she would join me under the mango tree. She had been quiet for almost an hour, and now a slight pressure of her hand drew my eyes back to her face.

'What will we do now?' she said. 'When will you send me to school?'

'Not for a long time. First you must get well and strong. That is all that matters.' She didn't seem to hear me. I think she knew she was dying, but she did not resent its happening.

'Who will read to you under the tree?' she went on. 'Who will look after you?' she asked, with the solicitude of a grown woman.

'You will, Madhu. You are grown up now. There will be no one else to look after me.'

The old woman was standing at my shoulder. A hundred years—and little Madhu was slipping away. The woman took Madhu's hand from mine, and laid it gently down. I sat by the cot a little longer, and then I rose to go, all the loneliness in the world pressing upon my heart.

ALL CREATURES GREAT AND SMALL

Instead of having brothers and sisters to grow up with in India, I had as my companions an odd assortment of pets, which included a monkey, a tortoise, a python and a Great Indian Hornbill. The person responsible for all this wildlife in the home was my grandfather. As the house was his own, other members of the family could not prevent him from keeping a large variety of pets, though they could certainly voice their objections; and as most of the household consisted of women—my grandmother, visiting aunts and occasional in-laws (my parents were in Burma at the time)—Grandfather and I had to be alert and resourceful in dealing with them. We saw eye to eye on the subject of pets, and whenever Grandmother decided it was time to get rid of a tame white rat or a squirrel, I would conceal them in a hole in the jackfruit tree; but unlike my aunts, she was generally tolerant of Grandfather's hobby, and even took a liking to some of our pets.

Grandfather's house and menagerie were in Dehra and I remember travelling there in a horse-drawn buggy. There were cars in those days—it was just over twenty years ago—but in the foothills a tonga was just as good, almost as fast, and certainly more dependable when it came to getting across the swift little Tons River.

During the rains, when the river flowed strong and deep, it was impossible to get across except on a hand-operated ropeway; but in the dry months, the horse went splashing through, the carriage wheels churning through clear mountain water. If the horse found the going difficult, we removed our shoes, rolled up our skirts or trousers, and waded across.

When Grandfather first went to stay in Dehra, early in the century, the only way of getting there was by the night mail coach. Mail ponies, he told me, were difficult animals, always attempting to turn around and get into the coach with the passengers. It was only when the coachman used his whip liberally, and reviled the ponies' ancestors as far back as their third and fourth generations, that the beasts could he persuaded to move. And once they started, there was no stopping them. It was a gallop all the way to the first stage, where the ponies were changed to the accompaniment of a bugle blown by the coachman.

At one stage of the journey, drums were beaten; and if it was night, torches were lit to keep away the wild elephants who, resenting the approach of this clumsy caravan, would sometimes trumpet a challenge and throw the ponies into confusion.

♦

Grandfather disliked dressing up and going out, and was only too glad to send everyone shopping or to the pictures—Harold Lloyd and Eddie Cantor were the favourites at Dehra's small cinema—so that he could be left alone to feed his pets and potter about in the garden. There were a lot of animals to be fed, including, for a time, a pair of Great Danes who had such enormous appetites that we were forced to give them away to a more affluent family.

The Great Danes were gentle creatures, and I would sit astride one of them and go for rides round the garden. Inspite of their size, they were very sure-footed and never knocked over people or chairs. A little monkey, like Toto, did much more damage.

Grandfather bought Toto from a tonga-owner for the sum of five rupees. The tonga-man used to keep the little, red monkey tied to a feed-trough, and Toto looked so out of place there—almost conscious of his own incongruity—that Grandfather immediately decided to add him to our menagerie.

Toto was really a pretty, little monkey. His bright eyes sparkled with mischief beneath deep-set eyebrows, and his teeth, a pearly-white, were often on display in a smile that frightened the life out of elderly Ango-Indian ladies. His hands were not those of a Tallulah Bankhead (Grandfather's only favourite actress), but were shrivelled and dried-up, as though they had been pickled in the sun for many years. But his fingers were quick and restless; and his tail, while adding to his good looks—Grandfather maintained that a tail would add to anyone's good looks—often performed the service of a third hand. He could use it to hang from a branch; and it was capable of scooping up any delicacy that might be out of the reach of his hands.

Grandmother, anticipating an outcry from other relatives,

always raised objections when Grandfather brought home some new bird or animal; and so for a while we managed to keep Toto's presence a secret by lodging him in a little closet opening into my bedroom wall. But in a few hours he managed to dispose of Grandmother's ornamental wallpaper and the better part of my school blazer. He was transferred to the stables for a day or two, and then Grandfather had to make a trip to neighbouring Saharanpur to collect his railway pension. Anxious to keep Toto out of trouble, he decided to take the monkey along with him.

Unfortunately I could not accompany Grandfather on this trip, but he told me about it afterwards.

A black kitbag was provided for Toto. When the strings of the bag were tied, there was no means of escape from within, and the canvas was too strong for Toto to bite his way through. His initial efforts to get out only had the effect of making the bag roll about on the floor, or occasionally jump in the air—an exhibition that attracted a curious crowd of onlookers on the Dehra railway platform.

Toto remained in the bag as far as Saharanpur, but while Grandfather was producing his ticket at the railway turnstile, Toto managed to get his hands through the aperture where the bag was tied, loosened the strings, and suddenly thrust his head through the opening.

The poor ticket-collector was visibly alarmed; but with great presence of mind, and much to the annoyance of Grandfather, he said, 'Sir, you have a dog with you. You'll have to pay for it accordingly.'

In vain did Grandfather take Toto out of the bag to prove that a monkey was not a dog or even a quadruped. The ticket-collector, now thoroughly annoyed, insisted on categorizing Toto as a dog; and three rupees and four annas had to be handed over as his fare. Then Grandfather, out of sheer spite, took out from his pocket a live tortoise that he happened to have with him, and said, 'What must I pay for this, since you charge for all animals?'

The ticket-collector retreated a pace or two; then advancing again with caution, he subjected the tortoise to a grave and knowledgeable stare.

'No ticket is necessary, sir,' he finally declared. 'There is no charge for insects.'

◆

When we discovered that Toto's favourite pastime was catching mice, we were able to persuade Grandmother to let us keep him. The unsuspecting mice would emerge from their holes at night to pick up any corn left over by our pony; and to get at it they had to run the gauntlet of Toto's section of the stable. He knew this, and would pretend to be asleep, keeping, however, one eye open. A mouse would make a rush—in vain; Toto, as swift as a cat, would have his paws upon him... Grandmother decided to put his talents to constructive use by tying him up one night in the larder, where a guerrilla-band of mice were playing havoc with our food supplies.

Toto was removed from his comfortable bed of straw in the stable, and chained up in the larder, beneath shelves of jam pots and other delicacies. The night was a long and miserable one for Toto, who must have wondered what he had done to deserve such treatment. The mice scampered about the place, while he, most uncatlike, lay curled up in a soup tureen, trying to snatch some sleep. At dawn, the mice returned to their holes; Toto awoke, scratched himself, emerged from the soup tureen, and looked about for something to eat. The jam pots attracted his notice, and it did not take him long to prise open the covers. Grandmother's treasured jams—she had made most of them herself—disappeared in an amazingly short time. I was present when she opened the door to see how many mice Toto had caught. Even the rain-god Indra could not have looked more terrible when planning a thunderstorm; and the imprecations Grandmother hurled at Toto were surprising coming from someone who had been brought up in the genteel Victorian manner.

The monkey was later reinstated in Grandmother's favour. A great treat for him on cold winter evenings was the large bowl of warm water provided by Grandmother for his bath. He would bathe himself, first of all gingerly testing the temperature of the water with his fingers. Leisurely he would step into the bath, first one foot, then the other, as he had seen me doing, until he was completely sitting down in it. Once comfortable, he would take the soap in his hands or feet, and rub himself all over. When he found the water becoming cold, he would get out and run as quickly as he could to the fire, where his coat soon dried. If anyone laughed at him during this performance, he would look extremely hurt, and refuse to go on with his ablutions.

One day Toto nearly succeeded in boiling himself to death.

The large kitchen kettle had been left on the fire to boil for tea; and Toto, finding himself for a few minutes alone with it, decided to take the lid off. On discovering that the water inside was warm, he got into the kettle with the intention of having a bath, and sat down with his head protruding from the opening. This was very pleasant for some time, until the water began to simmer. Toto raised himself a little, but finding it cold outside, sat down again. He continued standing and sitting for some time, not having the courage to face the cold air. Had it not been for the timely arrival of Grandmother, he would have been cooked alive.

If there is a part of the brain especially devoted to mischief, that part must have been largely developed in Toto. He was always tearing things to bits, and whenever one of my aunts came near him, he made every effort to get hold of her dress and tear a hole in it. A variety of aunts frequently came to stay with my grandparents, but during Toto's stay they limited their visits to a day or two, much to Grandfather's relief and Grandmother's annoyance.

Toto, however, took a liking to Grandmother, inspite of the beatings he often received from her. Whenever she allowed him the liberty, he would lie quietly in her lap instead of scrambling all over her as he did on most people.

Toto lived with us for over a year, but the following winter, after too much bathing, he caught pneumonia. Grandmother wrapped him in flannel, and Grandfather gave him a diet of chicken soup and Irish stew; but Toto did not recover. He was buried in the garden, under his favourite mango tree.

◆

Perhaps it was just as well that Toto was no longer with us when Grandfather brought home the python, or his demise might have been less conventional. Small monkeys are a favourite delicacy with pythons.

Grandmother was tolerant of most birds and animals, but she drew the line at reptiles. She said they made her blood run cold. Even a handsome, sweet-tempered chameleon had to be given up. Grandfather should have known that there was little chance of his being allowed to keep the python. It was about four feet long, a young one, when Grandfather bought it from a snake charmer for six rupees, impressing the bazaar crowd by slinging it across his shoulders and walking home with it. Grandmother nearly fainted at the sight of the python curled round Grandfather's throat.

'You'll be strangled!' she cried. 'Get rid of it at once!'

'Nonsense,' said Grandfather. 'He's only a young fellow. He'll soon get used to us.'

'Will he, indeed?' said Grandmother. But I have no intention of getting used to him. You know quite well that your cousin Mabel is coming to stay with us tomorrow. She'll leave us the minute she knows there's a snake in the house.'

'Well, perhaps we ought to show it to her as soon as she arrives,' said Grandfather, who did not look forward to fussy Aunt Mabel's visits any more than I did.

'You'll do no such thing,' said Grandmother.

'Well, I can't let it loose in the garden,' said Grandfather with an innocent expression. 'It might find its way into the poultry house, and then where would we be?'

'How exasperating you are!' grumbled Grandmother. 'Lock the creature in the bathroom, go back to the bazaar and find the man you bought it from, and get him to come and take it back.'

In my awestruck presence, Grandfather had to take the python into the bathroom, where he placed it in a steep-sided tin tub. Then he hurried off to the bazaar to look for the snake charmer, while Grandmother paced anxiously up and down the verandah. When he returned looking crestfallen, we knew he hadn't been able to find the man.

'You had better take it away yourself,' said Grandmother, in a relentless mood. 'Leave it in the jungle across the riverbed.'

'All right, but let me give it a feed first,' said Grandfather; and producing a plucked chicken, he took it into the bathroom, followed, in single file, by me, Grandmother and a curious cook and gardener.

Grandfather threw open the door and stepped into the bathroom. I peeped round his legs, while the others remained well behind. We couldn't see the python anywhere.

'He's gone,' announced Grandfather. 'He must have felt hungry.'

'I hope he isn't too hungry,' I said.

'We left the window open,' said Grandfather, looking embarrassed.

A careful search was made of the house, the kitchen, the garden, the stable and the poultry shed; but the python couldn't be found anywhere.

'He'll be well away by now,' said Grandfather reassuringly.

'I certainly hope so,' said Grandmother, who was halfway between anxiety and relief.

Aunt Mabel arrived next day for a three-week visit, and for a couple of days Grandfather and I were a little apprehensive in case the python made a sudden reappearance; but on the third day, when he didn't show up, we felt confident that he had gone for good.

And then, towards evening, we were startled by a scream

from the garden. Seconds later, Aunt Mabel came flying up the verandah steps, looking as though she had seen a ghost.

'In the guava tree!' she gasped. 'I was reaching for a guava, when I saw it staring at me. The *look* in its eyes! As though it would *devour* me—'

'Calm down, my dear,' urged Grandmother, sprinkling her with eau de cologne. 'Calm down and tell us what you saw.'

'A snake!' sobbed Aunt Mabel. 'A great boa constrictor. It must have been twenty feet long! In the guava tree. Its eyes were terrible. It looked at me in such a *queer* way...'

My grandparents looked significantly at each other, and Grandfather said, 'I'll go out and kill it,' and sheepishly taking hold of an umbrella, sallied out into the garden. But when he reached the guava tree, the python had disappeared.

'Aunt Mabel must have frightened it away,' I said.

'Hush,' said Grandfather. 'We mustn't speak of your aunt in that way.' But his eyes were alive with laughter.

After this incident, the python began to make a series of appearances, often in the most unexpected places. Aunt Mabel had another fit of hysterics when she saw him admiring her from under a cushion. She packed her bags, and Grandmother made us intensify the hunt.

Next morning I saw the python curled up on the dressing-table, gazing at his reflection in the mirror. I went for Grandfather, but by the time we returned the python had moved elsewhere. A little later he was seen in the garden again. Then he was back on the dressing-table, admiring himself in the mirror. Evidently he had become enamoured with his own reflection. Grandfather observed that perhaps the attention he was receiving from everyone had made him a little conceited.

'He's trying to look better for Aunt Mabel,' I said; a remark that I instantly regretted, because Grandmother overheard it, and brought the flat of her broad hand down on my head.

'Well, now we know his weakness,' said Grandfather.

'Are you trying to be funny too?' demanded Grandmother, looking her most threatening.

'I only meant he was becoming very vain,' said Grandfather hastily. 'It should be easier to catch him now.'

He set about preparing a large cage with a mirror at one end. In the cage he left a juicy chicken and various other delicacies, and fitted up the opening with a trapdoor. Aunt Mabel had already left by the time we had this trap ready, but we had to go on with the project because we couldn't have the python prowling about the house indefinitely.

For a few days nothing happened, and then, as I was leaving for school one morning, I saw the python curled up in the cage. He had eaten everything left out for him, and was relaxing in front of the mirror with something resembling a smile on his face—if you can imagine a python smiling... I lowered the trapdoor gently, but the python took no notice; he was in raptures over his handsome reflection. Grandfather and the gardener put the cage in the pony trap, and made a journey to the other side of the riverbed. They left the cage in the jungle, with the trapdoor open.

'He made no attempt to get out,' said Grandfather later. 'And I didn't have the heart to take the mirror away. It's the first time I've seen a snake fall in love.'

◆

'And the frogs have sung their old song in the mud...' This

was Grandfather's favourite quotation from Virgil, and he used it whenever we visited the rainwater pond behind the house where there were quantities of mud and frogs and the occasional water buffalo. Grandfather had once brought a number of frogs into the house. He had put them in a glass jar, left them on a windowsill, and then forgotten all about them. At about four o' clock in the morning the entire household was awakened by a loud and fearful noise, and Grandmother and several nervous relatives gathered in their nightclothes on the verandah. Their timidity changed to fury when they discovered that the ghastly sounds had come from Grandfather's frogs. Seeing the dawn breaking, the frogs had with one accord begun their morning song.

Grandmother wanted to throw the frogs, jar and all, out of the window; but Grandfather said that if he gave the jar a good shaking, the frogs would remain quiet. He was obliged to keep awake, in order to shake the bottle whenever the frogs showed any inclination to break into song. Fortunately for all concerned, the next day a servant took the top off the bottle to see what was inside. The sight of several big frogs so startled him that he ran off without replacing the cover; the frogs jumped out and presumably found their way back to the pond.

It became a habit with me to visit the pond on my own, in order to explore its banks and shallows. Taking off my shoes, I would wade into the muddy water up to my knees, to pluck the water lilies that floated on the surface.

One day I found the pond already occupied by several buffaloes. Their keeper, a boy a little older than me, was swimming about in the middle. Instead of climbing out on to the bank, he would pull himself up on the back of one of his buffaloes, stretch his naked brown body out on the animal's glistening wet hide, and start singing to himself.

When he saw me staring at him from across the pond, he smiled, showing gleaming white teeth in a dark, sun-burnished face. He invited me to join him in a swim. I told him I couldn't swim, and he offered to teach me. I hesitated, knowing that Grandmother held strict and old-fashioned views about mixing with village children; but, deciding that Grandfather—who sometimes smoked a hookah on the sly—would get me out of any trouble that might occur, I took the bold step of accepting the boy's offer. Once taken, the step did not seem so bold.

He dived off the back of his buffalo, and swam across to me. And I, having removed my clothes, followed his instructions until I was floundering about among the water lilies. His name was Ramu, and he promised to give me swimming lessons every afternoon; and so it was during the afternoons— especially summer afternoons when everyone was asleep—that we usually met. Before long I was able to swim across the pond to sit with Ramu astride a contented buffalo, the great beast standing like an island in the middle of a muddy ocean.

Sometimes we would try racing the buffaloes, Ramu and I sitting on different mounts. But they were lazy creatures, and would leave one comfortable spot only to look for another; or, if they were in no mood for games, would roll over on their backs, taking us with them into the mud and green slime of the pond. Emerging in shades of green and khaki, I would slip into the house through the bathroom, bathing under the tap before getting into my clothes.

One afternoon Ramu and I found a small tortoise in the

mud, sitting over a hole in which it had laid several eggs. Ramu kept the eggs for his dinner, and I presented the tortoise to Grandfather. He had a weakness for tortoises, and was pleased with this addition to his menagerie, giving it a large tub of water all to itself, with an island of rocks in the middle. The tortoise, however, was always getting out of the tub and wandering about the house. As it seemed able to look after itself quite well, we did not interfere. If one of the dogs bothered it too much, it would draw its head and legs into its shell, and defy all their attempts at rough play.

Ramu came from a family of bonded labourers, and had received no schooling. But he was well-versed in folklore, and knew a great deal about birds and animals.

'Many birds are sacred,' said Ramu, as we watched a bluejay swoop down from a peepul tree and carry off a grasshopper. He told me that both the bluejay and Lord Shiva were called 'Nilkanth'. Shiva had a blue throat, like the bird, because out of compassion for the human race he had swallowed a deadly poison which was intended to destroy the world. Keeping the poison in his throat, he did not let it go any further.

'Are squirrels sacred?' I asked, seeing one sprint down the trunk of the peepul tree.

'Oh yes, Lord Krishna loved squirrels,' said Ramu. 'He would take them in his arms and stroke them with his long fingers. That is why they have four dark lines down their backs from head to tail. Krishna was very dark, and the lines are the marks of his fingers.

Both Ramu and Grandfather were of the opinion that we should be more gentle with birds and animals, and should not kill so many of them.

'It is also important that we respect them,' said Grandfather. 'We must acknowledge their rights. Everywhere, birds and animals are finding it more difficult to survive, because we are trying to destroy both them and their forests. They have to keep moving as the trees disappear.'

This was especially true of the forests near Dehra, where the tiger and the pheasant and the spotted deer were beginning to disappear.

Ramu and I spent many long summer afternoons at the pond. I still remember him with affection, though we never saw each other again after I left Dehra. He could not read or write, so we were unable to keep in touch. And neither his people, nor mine, knew of our friendship. The buffaloes and frogs had been our only confidants. They had accepted us as part of their own world, their muddy but comfortable pond. And when I left Dehra, both they and Ramu must have assumed that I would return again like the birds.

A LOVE OF LONG AGO

Last week, as the taxi took me to Delhi, I passed through the small town in the foothills where I had lived as a young man.

Well, it's the only road to Delhi and one must go that way, but I seldom travel beyond the foothills. As the years go by, my visits to the city—any city—are few and far between. But whenever I am on that road, I look out of the window of my bus or taxi, to catch a glimpse of the first-floor balcony where a row of potted plants lend colour to an old and decrepit building. Ferns, a palm, a few bright marigolds, zinnias and nasturtiums—they made that balcony stand out from others; it was impossible to miss it.

But last week, when I looked out of the taxi window, the balcony garden had gone. A few broken pots remained; but the ferns had crumpled into dust, the palm had turned brown and yellow, and of the flowers nothing remained.

All these years I had taken that balcony garden for granted, and now it had gone. It jerked me upright in my seat. I looked back at the building for signs of life, but saw none. The taxi sped on. On my way back, I decided, I would look again. But it was as though a part of my life had come to an abrupt end; a part that I had almost come to take for granted. The link between youth and middle age, the bridge that spanned that gap, had suddenly been swept away.

And what had happened to Kamla, I wondered. Kamla, who had tended those plants all these years, knowing I would be looking out for them even though I might not see her, even though she might never see me.

Chance gives, and takes away, and gives again. But I would have to look elsewhere now, for the memories of my love, my young love, the girl who came into my life for a few blissful weeks and then went out of it for the remainder of our lives.

Was it almost thirty years ago that it all happened? How old was I then? Twenty-two at the most! And Kamla could not have been more than seventeen.

She had a laughing face, mischievous, always ready to break into a smile or peals of laughter. Sparkling brown eyes. How can I ever forget those eyes? Peeping at me from behind a window curtain, following me as I climbed the steps to my room—the room that was separated from her quarters by a narrow wooden landing that creaked loudly if I tried to move quietly across it. The trick was to dash across, as she did so neatly on her butterfly feet.

She was always on the move—flitting about on the verandah, running errands of no consequence, dancing on the steps, singing on the rooftop as she hung out the family washing. Only once was she still. That was when we met on the steps in the dark, and I stole a kiss, a sweet phantom kiss. She was very still then, very close, a butterfly drawing out nectar, and then she broke away from me and ran away laughing.

'What is your work?' she asked me one day.

'I write stories.'

'Will you write one about me?'

'Some day.'

I was living in a room above Moti-Bibi's grocery shop near the cinema. At night I could hear the soundtrack from the films. The songs did not help me much with my writing, nor with my affair, for Kamla could not come out at night. We met in the afternoons when the whole town took a siesta and expected us to do the same. Kamla had a young brother who worked for Moti-Bibi (a widow who was also my landlady) and it was through the boy that I had first met Kamla.

Moti-Bibi always a sent me a glass of kanji or sugar-cane juice or lime-juice (depending on the season) around noon. Usually the boy brought me the drink, but one day I looked up from my typewriter to see what at first I thought was an apparition hovering over me. She seemed to shimmer before me in the hot sunlight that came slashing through the open door. I looked up into her face and our eyes met over the rim of the glass. I forgot to take it from her.

What I liked about her was her smile. It dropped over her face slowly, like sunshine moving over brown hills. She seemed to give out some of the glow that was in her face. I felt it pour over me. And this golden feeling did not pass when she left the room. That was how I knew she was going to mean something special to me.

They were poor, but in time I was to realize that I was even poorer. When I discovered that plans were afoot to marry her to a widower of forty, I plucked up enough courage to declare that I would marry her myself. But my youth was no consideration. The widower had land and a generous gift of money for Kamla's parents. Not only was this offer attractive; it was customary. What had I to offer? A small rented room, a typewriter and a precarious income of two to three hundred rupees a month from freelancing. I told the brother that I would be famous one day, that I would be rich, that I would be writing bestsellers! He did not believe me. And who can blame him? I never did write bestsellers or become rich. Nor did I have parents or relatives to speak on my behalf.

I thought of running away with Kamla. When I mentioned it to her, her eyes lit up. She thought it would be great fun. Women in love can be more reckless than men! But I had read too many stories about runaway marriages ending in disaster, and I lacked the courage to go through with such an adventure. I must have known instinctively that it would not work. Where would we go, and how would we live? There would be no home to crawl back to, for either of us.

Had I loved more passionately, more fiercely, I might have felt compelled to elope with Kamla, regardless of the consequences. But it never became an intense relationship. We had so few moments together. Always stolen moments—on the stairs, on the roof, in the deserted junkyard behind the shops. She seemed to enjoy every moment of this secret affair. I fretted and longed for something more permanent. Her responses, so sweet and generous, only made my longing greater. But she seemed content with the immediate moment and what it offered.

And so the marriage took place, and she did not appear to be too dismayed about her future. But before she left for her husband's house, she asked me for some of the plants that I had owned and nourished on my small balcony.

'Take them all,' I said. 'I am leaving, anyway.'

'Where are you going?'

'To Delhi—to find work. But I shall come this way sometimes.'

'My husband's house is on the Delhi road. You will pass that way. I will keep these flowers where you can see them.'

We did not touch each other in parting. Her brother came and collected the plants. Only the cacti remained. Not a lover's plant, the cactus! I gave the cacti to my landlady and went to live in Delhi.

♦

And whenever I passed through the old place, summer or winter, I looked out of the window of my bus or taxi and saw the garden flourishing on Kamla's balcony; leaf and fern abounded, and the flowers grew rampant on the sunny ledge.

Once I saw her, leaning over the balcony railing. I stopped the taxi and waved to her. She waved back, smiling like the sun breaking through clouds. She called to me to come up, but I said I would come another time. I never did visit her home, and I never saw her husband. Her parents had gone back to their village, her brother had vanished into the great grey spaces of India.

In recent years, after leaving Delhi and making my home in the hills, I have passed through the town less often; but the flowers have always been there, bright and glowing in their increasingly shabby surroundings. Except on this last journey of mine...

And on the return trip, only yesterday, I looked again, but the house was empty and desolate. I got out of the car and looked up at the balcony and called Kamla's name—called it after so many years—but there was no answer.

I asked questions in the locality. The old man had died, his wife had gone away, probably to her village. There had been no children. Would she return? No one could say. The house had been sold; it would be pulled down to make way for a block of flats.

I glanced once more at the deserted balcony, the withered, drooping plants. A butterfly flitted about the railing, looking in vain for a flower on which to alight. It settled briefly on my hand, before opening its wings and fluttering away into the blue.

THE BAR THAT TIME FORGOT

'Cockroaches!' exclaimed Her Highness the Maharani. 'Cockroaches everywhere! Can't put down my glass without finding a cockroach beneath it!'

'Cockroaches have a special liking for this room,' observed Colonel Wilkie, from his corner by the disused fireplace. 'For one thing, our Melaram there—' and he indicated the bartender with a tilt of his double chin—'never washes the glasses properly. And there are sandwich remains all over the place. Last week's sandwiches, I might add. From that party of yours, Krishan.'

Krishan, former Test cricketer, now forty and with a forty-three-inch waist, turned to the colonel. 'You should see the kitchen. A pigsty. The cook is seldom sober.'

'*We* are seldom sober,' said Suresh Mathur, income-tax lawyer, from his favourite bar stool.

'Speak for yourself,' snapped H.H. 'Simon, fetch me another whisky.'

Simon Lee, secretary-companion to Her Highness, rose dutifully from his chair and took her glass over to the bar counter.

'Indian whisky or Scotch, sir?' asked the bartender in a loud voice, knowing the Maharani was too mean to buy Scotch.

'Whisky will do,' said Simon. 'And a beer for me.' Just then he felt like spiking the Maharani's whisky with something really lethal, and be free of her for the rest of his days. Years of loyalty and companionship had given way to abject slavery, and there was nothing he could do about it. Nearing seventy, unqualified and unworldly, he could hardly set about creating any sort of career for himself.

'And what are *you* having?' he asked Suresh Mathur, who had just put away his first drink.

'I am never vague, I ask for Haig!' Suresh replied, chuckling at his clever rhyme. None of the others thought it amusing, but this was usual. 'When they stop giving me credit, I'll try the local stuff.'

'Good on you!' called Colonel Wilkie from his corner. 'But there's nothing to beat Solan No. 1. Don't trust these single malts—they always give one gout!'

'I've never seen you move from that chair,' said Krishan. 'No wonder you suffer from gout.'

'Played cricket once, like you,' said the Colonel. 'Made a few runs. But they always made me twelfth man. Got fed up of carrying out the drinks, or fielding when the star batsman felt indisposed. Gave up cricket. Indoor games are better. Why don't we have a dartboard in here? In England, every respectable pub has a dartboard.'

I'd been listening to the conversation from a small table behind a potted palm. I was sixteen, just out of school, and I wasn't supposed to be in the bar, even if I wasn't drinking. The large potted palm separated the bar-room from the outer lounge; it was neutral territory.

'I have a dartboard!' I piped up, and every head turned towards me. Most of them had been unaware of my presence. They knew, of course, that I was the son of the lady who managed the hotel.

Suresh Mathur, the most literary-inclined of the lot, said: 'Young Copperfield has a dartboard!'

'I'll go and fetch it,' I said, only too ready to justify my presence in the bar.

I dashed down the corridor to my room and collided with my mother who was doing her nightly round of the hotel.

'What are you doing here? You mustn't hang around the bar,' she said sharply. 'You have a radio in your room, apart from all your books.'

The radio had been given to me the previous year by a guest who was now wanted by the police (on suspicion of being a serial killer), but I did not feel in any way guilty about possessing it; the guest had been very friendly and generous.

'Darts,' I told my mother. 'They want to play darts. That's what a pub is for, isn't it?' And I charged into my room, picked up my old dartboard and set of darts, and returned breathless to the bar-room.

My arrival was greeted by cheers, and Krishan helped me find a place for the dartboard, just below a framed picture of winged cherubs sporting about on some unlikely clouds.

'Whoever gets the highest score gets a free drink,' announced Krishan.

'Who pays for it?' asked Suresh Mathur.

'We all do—income-tax lawyers included.'

'He never saved anyone a rupee of tax,' declared the

Maharani. 'But come on, let's have a game.'

'Would you like to start the proceedings, H.H.?'

'No, I'll wait till everyone's finished. You can start with Colonel Wilkie.'

'Age before beauty,' said Krishan. 'Come on, Colonel, we know you have a steady hand.'

Colonel Wilkie's hand was far from steady. His hands were always trembling. But he struggled out of his chair and took up his position at a point indicated by Krishan. Only one of his darts struck the board, earning him fifteen points. The others were near misses. Two darts bounced off the picture on the wall.

'The old fool's aiming at those naked cherubs,' crowed H.H. 'Go on, Simon, see if you can win a free drink for me.'

Simon did his best, but scored a meagre thirty points.

'Idiot!' cried H.H. 'And you always said you were a good darts player.'

'Out of practice,' Simon mumbled.

Meanwhile, someone had opened up the old radiogram and placed a record on the turntable. The cheeky voice of Maurice Chevalier filled the room:

All I want is just one girl,
But I have to have one girl
All I want is one
For a start!

The evening was livening up. Suresh Mathur scored a few points, but it was Krishan who hit the bullseye and claimed a drink on the house.

'Not until I've had my turn,' shouted H.H., and made a grab for the darts.

She flung them at the board at random, missing wildly—so much so that one dart lodged itself in Colonel Wilkie's old felt hat which was hanging from a peg, while another streaked across the room and narrowly missed the Roman nose of Reggie Bhowmik, ex-actor, who had just entered the room accompanied by his demure little wife.

Between ex-actor Reggie and former cricketer Krishan there was no love lost. Both middle aged and no longer in demand, they were rivals in failure. One spoke of the prejudice and incompetence of the cricket selectors, the other of jealousy in the film industry and his subsequent neglect. Both lived in the past—Krishan recalling the one outstanding innings he had played for the country (before being dropped after a series of failures), Reggie living on memories of his one great romantic role before a sagging waistline and alcohol-coarsened features had led to a rapid decline in his popularity. Somehow they had drifted into the backwater that was Dehra in 1950.

There are some places, no matter how dull or lacking in opportunity, which nevertheless take a grip on the individual, especially the more easy-going types, and hold him in thrall, rendering him unfit for life in a larger, more competitive milieu. Dehra was one such place.

The bar at Green's Hotel was their refuge and their strength. Here they could reminisce, hark back to glory days, even speak optimistically of the future. Colonel Wilkie, Suresh Mathur, Krishan Kapoor, Reggie Bhowmik, H.H.—the Maharani—and Simon Lee, were all dropouts, failures in their own way. Had they been busy and successful, they would not have found their way to Green's every evening.

Reggie Bhowmik liked making dramatic entrances, but the

Maharani was just as fond of being the centre of attention, and wasn't about to give up centre stage to a fading actor.

'A double whisky for Krishan!' she declared. 'He's the only one here who still has a steady hand.'

'You haven't felt *my* hand,' said Reggie, bearing down on her. 'You missed my nose by a whisker.'

'You'd look better with a scar running down your face,' said H.H. 'Then you might get a role as Frankenstein or the phantom of the opera.'

This touched a raw nerve, as Reggie had been having some difficulty in getting a decent role in recent months. But he snapped back: 'I'll play the phantom on condition that you're cast as the fat soprano—then I shall take great pleasure in strangling you.'

'Let's change the subject,' said his wife Ruby, always ready to pour oil on troubled waters. She moved over to Colonel Wilkie's table and asked: 'How have you been, Colonel?'

'Like an old bus just about moving, and badly in need of spare parts.'

'Well, have a beer with us—and some French fries if we can get any.'

'Cook's on strike,' said Krishan. 'Only liquid diet today.' I saw my opportunity, and piped up again from behind the potted palm. 'I can boil some eggs for you if you like!' There was a stunned silence, broken by Suresh Mathur who said, sounding a little incredulous, 'Young Master Copperfield can boil an egg!'

Everyone clapped, and Krishan said, 'Copperfield has certainly saved the day for us. First he produces a dartboard, and now he's about to save us from starvation. Go to it, Copperfield!'

Off I went, then, not to boil eggs—there weren't any in the kitchen—but to find Sitaram, the room-boy, who was the only person of my age in the hotel. I found him in my room, listening to 'Binaca Geetmala', the popular musical request programme, on my radio.

'We need some eggs,' I told him. 'Boiled.'

'Egg-man comes tomorrow,' he said. 'Cook finished the rest. Made himself an omelette, got drunk, and took off!'

'Well, let's go down to the bazaar and buy some eggs. I've got enough money on me.'

So off we went, and near the clock tower found a street vendor selling boiled eggs. We bought a dozen and hurried back to the bar-room, where Krishan and Reggie were having a heated argument on the relative merits of cricket and football. Reggie didn't think much of cricket, and Krishan didn't think much of football.

'And what's *your* favourite game?' asked Ruby of Suresh Mathur.

'Snakes and ladders,' he said, chuckling, and returned to his drink.

'Boiled eggs!' I announced. 'On the house!'

Sitaram produced saucers, and distributed the eggs among the guests—two each, exactly.

'Do I have to peel my own egg?' asked the Maharani querulously, staring down at the two eggs rolling about on her plate. 'Peel them for me, Simon!'

Simon dutifully cracked one of the eggs and began peeling it for her. 'Not that way, you fool. You're leaving all the skin on it.' And seizing the half-peeled egg from her companion, she flung it across the room, narrowly missing the bartender.

'Good throw!' exclaimed Krishan. 'You'd be great fielding on the boundary.'

'Better at baseball,' said Reggie.

'Snakes and ladders,' said Suresh again, now quite drunk.

Colonel Wilkie, equally drunk, gave a loud belch.

The Maharani got up to leave. 'Well, I'm not going to sit here to be insulted by everyone. Come on, Simon, drive me home!' And she marched out of the room with an attempt at majesty, but tripped over the hotel cat, an ugly, striped creature who had sensed that there was food around and had come looking for it. The cat caterwauled, H.H. screamed and cursed, Reggie cheered, and Suresh Mather pronounced, 'When two cats are fighting they make a hideous sound.'

Not to be outdone in nastiness, the Maharani went up to Suresh, looked him up and down, and said, 'It's easy to tell you're a single man.'

'I'm not homosexual,' said Suresh defensively. (The word 'gay' had yet to be used in any sense other than 'happy' in those days.)

'No,' the Maharani smiled wickedly. 'You're single because you are so damn ugly!'

And on that triumphant note she left the room, followed by the obedient Simon.

'Pay no attention to her, Suresh,' said Krishan generously. 'You're better-looking than that old lapdog who follows her around.'

'I understand she's leaving him her fortunes,' said Reggie. 'I could do with some of it myself. Perhaps I could interest her in producing a film.'

'She's tight-fisted,' said Krishan. 'If you look closely at

Simon you'll notice he's wearing the late Maharaja's smoking jacket and deerstalker cap. The old Maharaja loved dressing up like Sherlock Holmes.'

Colonel Wilkie came out of his reverie. 'When I was in Jamnagar—' he began.

'We've heard that a hundred times,' said Krishan.

'*I* haven't,' said Ruby.

'When I was in Jamnagar,' continued Colonel Wilkie, 'I saw Duleep Singh ji make a hundred. That was against Lord Tennyson's team.'

'Yesterday you said Ranjit Singh ji,' remarked Krishan.

'I'm not that old,' said Colonel Wilkie, struggling to his feet. 'But old enough to want to go to bed. I'll toddle off now.' Locating his walking-stick, he found his way to the door, wishing everyone goodnight as he passed them. They heard the tap of his walking stick as he walked away down the corridor.

'Shouldn't someone go with him?' asked Ruby. 'It's very late and he isn't too steady on his feet.'

'Oh, he'll find his way home,' said Suresh nonchalantly. 'Lives just around the corner, in rented rooms near the Club.'

'Why doesn't he join the Club?'

'Can't afford it. Neither can I.'

'Neither can I,' said Krishan.

'Neither can we,' added Ruby, sadly. 'And anyway, it's more homely here. Even when the Maharani is around.'

'*She* can afford the Club,' said Suresh. 'But they won't let her in. Created a disturbance once too often. Insulted the secretary and emptied a dish of chicken biryani on his head.'

'Not done,' said Krishan. 'Not cricket.'

'I don't believe it,' said Reggie. 'Can't be true.'

'Calling me a liar?' asked Suresh, bristling.

Ruby poured oil on troubled waters again. 'Interesting if true,' she said. 'And if not true, still interesting.'

'Mark Twain.'

My mother came along the corridor just as Krishan had shown off his knowledge of literature, and found me behind the palms listening to all this fascinating talk.

'Time you went to your room, young man,' she said.

'I'm waiting for everyone to go home,' I said. 'Then I'll help Sitaram tidy up. There's no cook, as you know.'

'Let him stay,' called Suresh from his bar stool. 'It's all part of his education. And he's old enough for a glass of beer. How old are you, sonny?'

'Sixteen,' I said.

'Well, enjoy yourself. It's later than you think.'

But I wasn't thinking of beer just then. I knew there were sausages in the fridge, and I had every intention of polishing them off as soon as all the guests had gone. I wanted to be a writer, but I had no intention of starving in a garret. However, all thoughts of food vanished when I looked across the room and saw Colonel Wilkie framed in the opposite doorway. He was staring at us through the glass. The glass door then opened of its own volition, and Colonel Wilkie stepped into the room. We all looked up, and Reggie said, 'Back again, Colonel? Still feeling thirsty?' But Colonel Wilkie ignored the jibe, and walked slowly across the room to the table where he had been sitting. This was close to where I was standing. He bent down and picked up his pipe from the table. He'd forgotten it when he'd left the bar-room. Shoving the pipe into his pocket, he turned and retraced his steps, leaving the room by the door from which he had entered.

'Well, I'm blowed,' said Krishan. 'I thought he was sleepwalking.'

'Never goes anywhere without his pipe,' said Suresh. 'A perfect example of single-mindedness.'

'Didn't say a word.'

'The pipe was all that mattered.'

'Like a favourite cricket bat,' said Krishan.

'Maybe I'll come back for mine when I'm dead.'

A silence fell upon the room. The mention of death had a sobering effect upon the small group. And come to think of it, Colonel Wilkie on his return to the bar-room had something of the zombie about him—the walking dead.

There was a commotion in the passageway, and my mother burst into the room, followed by the night-watchman.

'Colonel Wilkie's dead,' said my mother. 'He collapsed on his steps about half an hour ago.'

'But he was here five minutes ago,' said Krishan.

'No, sir,' said Gopal the watchman. 'I went home with him when he left here some time back. Madam said to keep an eye on him. When we got to his place, he began climbing his steps with some difficulty. I helped him to the top step, and then he collapsed. I dragged him into his room and then ran for Dr Bhist. He is there now.'

There was silence for a couple of minutes, and then Ruby said, 'We all saw him. Colonel Wilkie.'

'We saw his ghost,' Krishan murmured.

'He came for his pipe,' said Suresh quietly. 'I told you he wouldn't go anywhere without it.'

Colonel Wilkie was buried the next day, and we made

sure his pipe was buried with him. We did not want him turning up from time to time, looking for it. It could be a bit unnerving for the customers.

In all the excitement I'd forgotten about the sausages, but decided they would keep until after the funeral.

All the regular barflies turned up for the funeral. H.H. was quite sloshed when she arrived and had to be extricated from an open grave into which she had slipped, the ground being soft and yielding after recent rain. She blamed secretary Simon for the mishap and called him an *ullu ka patha*—son of an owl—but he was quite used to such broadsides and took them in his stride. Was it love or loyalty or dependence that kept him in abeyance? Or was it, as some said, the prospect of becoming her heir? If so, he was paying a heavy price well in advance of such a prospect. Not everyone relishes being abused and kicked around in public by a half-crazed maharani.

When Colonel Wilkie's coffin was lowered into the grave, we all said 'Cheers!' He would have liked that. We then returned to Green's for an early opening of the bar. Alcoholics Unanimous held a subdued but not too melancholy meeting.

But bad news was in store for everyone. A day or two later, I heard the owner, our Sardarji, inform my mother that the hotel had been sold and that she'd have to leave at the end of the month. She'd been expecting something like this, and had already accepted a matron's job at one of the schools in the valley. As for me, I was to be packed off to England to my aunt's home in Jersey. The prospect did not thrill me, but I was more or less resigned to it. And there did not appear to be much future for me in Dehra.

Even before the month was out, workers had begun pulling

down parts of the building. It was to be rebuilt as a cinema hall, and would show the latest hits from Bombay. It was even rumoured that Dilip Kumar, the biggest star of that era, would inaugurate the new cinema when it was ready to open.

The spirit and character of a building lasts only while the building lasts. Remove the roof-beams, pull down the walls, smash the stairways, and you are left with nothing but memories. Even the ghosts have nowhere to go.

An old hotel that once had a personality of its own was now dismantled with startling rapidity. It had gone up slowly, brick by brick; it came down like a house of cards. No treasures cascaded from its walls; no skeletons were discovered. In two or three days the demolishers had wiped out the past, removed Green's Hotel from the face of the earth so effectively that it might never have existed.

Searching through the ruins one day, I found a bottle-opener lying in the dust, and kept it as a souvenir.

The bar had been the only common factor in the lives of those disparate individuals who had come there so regularly—drawn to the place rather than to each other.

Now they went their different ways—Suresh Mathur to the Club, the Maharani to her card table and private bar, Krishan to a public school as a cricket coach, Reggie Bhowmik and Ruby to Darjeeling to make a documentary... Sitaram continued to work for my mother, so I had his company whenever he was free.

The cinema came up quite rapidly, but I had left for England before it opened. When I returned five years later, it was showing Madhubala and Guru Dutt in a romantic comedy, *Mr & Mrs 55*.

Then I moved to Delhi.

In recent years, some of the old single cinemas have been closing down, giving way to multiplexes. The other day, passing through Dehra, I saw that 'our' cinema hall was being pulled down. 'What now?' I asked my taxi driver. 'A multiplex?' 'No, sir. A shopping mall!'

And such is progress.

I think I'm the only one around who is old enough to remember the old Green's Hotel, its dusty corridors, shabby bar-room, and oddball customers. All have gone. All forgotten! Not even footprints in the sands of time. But by putting down this memoir of an evening or two at that forgotten watering place, I think I have cheated Time just a little.

THE LAST TONGA RIDE

It was a warm spring day in Dehra, and the walls of the bungalow were aflame with flowering bougainvillaea. The papayas were ripening. The scent of sweetpeas drifted across the garden. Grandmother sat in an easy chair in a shady corner of the verandah, her knitting needles clicking away, her head nodding now and then. She was knitting a pullover for my father. 'Delhi has cold winters,' she had said; and although the winter was still eight months away, she had set to work on getting our woollens ready.

In the Kathiawar states, touched by the warm waters of the Arabian Sea, it had never been cold but Dehra lies at the foot of the first range of the Himalayas.

Grandmother's hair was white, her eyes were not very strong but her fingers moved quickly with the needles and the needles kept clicking all morning.

When Grandmother wasn't looking, I picked geranium leaves, crushed them between my fingers and pressed them to my nose.

I had been in Dehra with my grandmother for almost a

month and I had not seen my father during this time. We had never before been separated for so long. He wrote to me every week, and sent me books and picture postcards; and I would walk to the end of the road to meet the postman as early as possible, to see if there was any mail for us.

We heard the jingle of tonga-bells at the gate, and a familiar horse-buggy came rattling up the drive.

'I'll see who's come,' I said, and ran down the verandah steps and across the garden.

It was Bansi Lal in his tonga. There were many tongas and tonga-drivers in Dehra but Bansi was my favourite driver. He was young and handsome and he always wore a clean white shirt and pyjamas. His pony, too, was bigger and faster than the other tonga ponies. Bansi didn't have a passenger, so I asked him, 'What have you come for, Bansi?'

'Your grandmother sent for me, dost.' He did not call me 'chota sahib' or 'baba', but 'dost' and this made me feel much more important. Not every small boy could boast of a tonga-driver for his friend!

'Where are you going, Granny?' I asked, after I had run back to the verandah.

'I'm going to the bank.'

'Can I come too?'

'Whatever for? What will you do in the bank?'

'Oh, I won't come inside, I'll sit in the tonga with Bansi.'

'Come along, then.'

We helped Grandmother into the back seat of the tonga, and then I joined Bansi in the driver's seat. He said something to his pony, and the pony set off at a brisk trot, out of the gate and down the road.

'Now, not too fast, Bansi,' said Grandmother, who didn't like anything that went too fast—tonga, motor car, train, or bullock-cart.

'Fast?' said Bansi. 'Have no fear, Memsahib. This pony has never gone fast in its life. Even if a bomb went off behind us, we could go no faster. I have another pony, which I use for racing when customers are in a hurry. This pony is reserved for you, Memsahib.'

There was no other pony, but Grandmother did not know this, and was mollified by the assurance that she was riding in the slowest tonga in Dehra.

A ten-minute ride brought us to the bazaar. Grandmother's bank, the Allahabad Bank, stood near the clock tower. She was gone for about half an hour and during this period Bansi and I sauntered about in front of the shops. The pony had been left with some green stuff to munch.

'Do you have any money on you?' asked Bansi.

'Four annas,' I said.

'Just enough for two cups of tea,' said Bansi, putting his arm round my shoulders and guiding me towards a tea stall. The money passed from my palm to his.

'You can have tea, if you like,' I said. 'I'll have a lemonade.'

'So be it, friend. A tea and a lemonade, and be quick about it,' said Bansi to the boy in the stall and presently the drinks were set before us and Bansi was making a sound rather like his pony when he drank, while I burped my way through some green, gaseous stuff that tasted more like soap than lemonade.

When Grandmother came out of the bank, she looked pensive, and did not talk much during the ride back to the house except to tell me to behave myself when I leaned over to pat the pony on its rump. After paying off Bansi, she marched straight indoors.

'When will you come again?' I asked Bansi.

'When my services are required, dost. I have to make a living, you know. But I tell you what, since we are friends, the next time I am passing this way after leaving a fare, I will jingle my bells at the gate and if you are free and would like a ride—a fast ride—you can join me. It won't cost you anything. Just bring some money for a cup of tea.'

'All right—since we are friends,' I said.

'Since we are friends.'

And touching the pony very lightly with the handle of his whip, he sent the tonga rattling up the drive and out of the gate. I could hear Bansi singing as the pony cantered down the road.

Ayah was waiting for me in the bedroom, her hands resting on her broad hips—sure sign of an approaching storm.

'So you went off to the bazaar without telling me,' she said. (It wasn't enough that I had Grandmother's permission!) 'And all this time I've been waiting to give you your bath.'

'It's too late now, isn't it?' I asked hopefully.

'No, it isn't. There's still an hour left for lunch. Off with your clothes!'

While I undressed, Ayah berated me for keeping the company of tonga-drivers like Bansi. I think she was a little jealous.

'He is a rogue, that man. He drinks, gambles and smokes opium. He has TB and other terrible diseases. So don't you be too friendly with him, understand, baba?'

I nodded my head sagely but said nothing. I thought Ayah

was exaggerating, as she always did about people, and besides, I had no intention of giving up free tonga rides.

As my father had told me, Dehra was a good place for trees, and Grandmother's house was surrounded by several kinds—peepul, seem, mango, jackfruit, papaya and an ancient banyan tree. Some of the trees had been planted by my father and grandfather.

'How old is the jackfruit tree?' I asked Grandmother.

'Now let me see,' said Grandmother, looking very thoughtful. 'I should remember the jackfruit tree. Oh yes, your grandfather put it down in 1927. It was during the rainy season. I remember, because it was your father's birthday and we celebrated it by planting a tree. 14 July 1927. Long before you were born!'

The banyan tree grew behind the house. Its spreading branches, which hung to the ground and took root again, formed a number of twisting passageways in which I liked to wander. The tree was older than the house, older than my grandparents, as old as Dehra. I could hide myself in its branches behind thick, green leaves and spy on the world below.

It was an enormous tree, about sixty feet high, and the first time I saw it I trembled with excitement because I had never seen such a marvellous tree before. I approached it slowly, even cautiously, as I wasn't sure the tree wanted my friendship. It looked as though it had many secrets. There were sounds and movement in the branches but I couldn't see who or what made the sounds.

The tree made the first move, the first overture of friendship. It allowed a leaf to fall.

The leaf brushed against my face as it floated down, but before it could reach the ground I caught and held it. I studied the leaf, running my fingers over its smooth, glossy texture. Then I put out my hand and touched the rough bark of the tree and this felt good to me. So I removed my shoes and socks as people do when they enter a holy place; and finding first a foothold and then a handhold on that broad trunk, I pulled myself up with the help of the tree's aerial roots.

As I climbed, it seemed as though someone was helping me; invisible hands, the hands of the spirit in the tree, touched me and helped me climb.

But although the tree wanted me, there were others who were disturbed and alarmed by my arrival. A pair of parrots suddenly shot out of a hole in the trunk and, with shrill cries, flew across the garden—flashes of green and red and gold. A squirrel looked out from behind a branch, saw me, and went scurrying away to inform his friends and relatives.

I climbed higher, looked up, and saw a red beak poised above my head. I shrank away, but the hornbill made no attempt to attack me. He was relaxing in his home, which was a great hole in the tree trunk. Only the bird's head and great beak were showing. He looked at me in a rather bored way, drowsily opening and shutting his eyes.

'So many creatures live here,' I said to myself. 'I hope none of them are dangerous!'

At that moment the hornbill lunged at a passing cricket. Bill and tree trunk met with a loud and resonant 'Tonk!'

I was so startled that I nearly fell out of the tree. But it was a difficult tree to fall out of! It was full of places where one could sit or even lie down. So I moved away from the hornbill, crawled along a branch which had sent out supports, and so moved quite a distance from the main body of the tree. I left its cold, dark depths for an area penetrated by shafts of sunlight.

No one could see me. I lay flat on the broad branch hidden by a screen of leaves. People passed by on the road below. A sahib in a sun-helmet. His memsahib twirling a coloured silk sun-umbrella. Obviously she did not want to get too brown and be mistaken for a country-born person. Behind them, a pram wheeled along by a nanny.

Then there were a number of Indians; some in white dhotis, some in western clothes, some in loincloths. Some with baskets on their heads. Others with coolies to carry their baskets for them.

A cloud of dust, the blare of a horn, and down the road, like an out-of-condition dragon, came the latest Morris touring car. Then cyclists. Then a man with a basket of papayas balanced on his head. Following him, a man with a performing monkey. This man rattled a little hand drum, and children followed the man and the monkey along the road. They stopped in the shade of a mango tree on the other side of the road. The little red monkey wore a frilled dress and a baby's bonnet. It danced for the children, while the man sang and played his drum.

The clip-clop of a tonga pony, and Bansi's tonga came rattling down the road. I called down to him and he reined in with a shout of surprise, and looked up into the branches of the banyan tree.

'What are you doing up there?' he cried.

'Hiding from Grandmother,' I said.

'And when are you coming for that ride?'

'On Tuesday afternoon,' I said.

'Why not today?'

'Ayah won't let me. But she has Tuesdays off.'

Bansi spat red paan juice across the road. 'Your ayah is jealous,' he said.

'I know,' I said. 'Women are always jealous, aren't they? I suppose it's because she doesn't have a tonga.'

'It's because she doesn't have a tonga-driver,' said Bansi, grinning up at me. 'Never mind. I'll come on Tuesday—that's the day after tomorrow, isn't it?'

I nodded down to him, and then started backing along my branch, because I could hear Ayah calling in the distance. Bansi leant forward and smacked his pony across the rump, and the tonga shot forward.

'What were you doing up there?' asked Ayah a little later.

'I was watching a snake cross the road,' I said. I knew she couldn't resist talking about snakes. There weren't as many in Dehra as there had been in Kathiawar and she was thrilled that I had seen one.

'Was it moving towards you or away from you?' she asked.

'It was going away.'

Ayah's face clouded over. 'That means poverty for the beholder,' she said gloomily.

Later, while scrubbing me down in the bathroom, she began to air all her prejudices, which included drunkards ('they die quickly anyway'), misers ('they get murdered sooner or later') and tonga-drivers ('they have all the vices').

'You are a very lucky boy,' she said suddenly, peering closely at my tummy.

'Why?' I asked. 'You just said I would be poor because I saw a snake going the wrong way.'

'Well, you won't be poor for long. You have a mole on your tummy, and that's very lucky. And there is one under your armpit, which means you will be famous. Do you have one on the neck? No, thank God! A mole on the neck is the sign of a murderer!'

'Do you have any moles?' I asked.

Ayah nodded seriously, and pulling her sleeve up to her shoulder, showed me a large mole high on her arm.

'What does that mean?' I asked.

'It means a life of great sadness,' said Ayah gloomily.

'Can I touch it ?' I asked.

'Yes, touch it,' she said, and taking my hand, she placed it against the mole.

'It's a nice mole,' I said, wanting to make Ayah happy. 'Can I kiss it?'

'You can kiss it,' said Ayah.

I kissed her on the mole.

'That's nice,' she said.

Tuesday afternoon came at last, and as soon as Grandmother was asleep and Ayah had gone to the bazaar, I was at the gate, looking up and down the road for Bansi and his tonga. He was not long in coming. Before the tonga turned into the road, I could hear his voice, singing to the accompaniment of the carriage bells. He reached down, took my hand, and hoisted me on to the seat beside him. Then we went off down the road at a steady jogtrot. It was only when we reached the outskirts of the town that Bansi encouraged his pony to greater efforts. He rose in his seat, leaned forward and slapped the pony across the haunches. From a brisk trot we changed to a carefree canter. The tonga swayed from side to side. I clung to Bansi's free arm, while he grinned at me, his mouth red with paan juice.

'Where shall we go, dost?' he asked.

'Nowhere,' I said. 'Anywhere.'

'We'll go to the river,' said Bansi.

The 'river' was really a swift mountain stream that ran through the forests outside Dehra, joining the Ganga about fifteen miles away. It was almost dry during the winter and early summer; in flood during the monsoon.

The road out of Dehra was a gentle decline and soon we were rushing headlong through the tea gardens and eucalyptus forests, the pony's hoofs striking sparks off the metalled road, the carriage wheels groaning and creaking so loudly that I feared one of them would come off and that we would all be thrown into a ditch or into the small canal that ran beside the road. We swept through mango groves, through guava and litchi orchards, past broad-leaved sal and shisham trees. Once in the sal forest, Bansi turned the tonga on to a rough cart track, and we continued along it for about a furlong, until the road dipped down to the stream bed.

'Let us go straight into the water,' said Bansi. 'You and I and the pony!' And he drove the tonga straight into the middle of the stream, where the water came up to the pony's knees.

'I am not a great one for baths,' said Bansi, 'but the pony needs one, and why should a horse smell sweeter than its owner?' Saying which, he flung off his clothes and jumped into the water.

'Better than bathing under a tap!' he cried, slapping himself on the chest and thighs. 'Come down, dost, and join me!'

After some hesitation I joined him, but had some difficulty in keeping on my feet in the fast current. I grabbed at the pony's tail, and hung on to it, while Bansi began sloshing water over the patient animal's back.

After this, Bansi led both me and the pony out of the stream and together we gave the carriage a good washing down. I'd had a free ride and Bansi got the services of a free helper for the long overdue spring cleaning of his tonga. After we had finished the job, he presented me with a packet of aam pafiat—a sticky toffee made from mango pulp—and for some time I tore at it as a dog tears at a hit of old leather. Then I felt drowsy and lay down on the brown, sun-warmed grass. Crickets and grasshoppers were telephoning each other from tree and bush and a pair of bluejays rolled, dived and swooped acrobatically overhead.

Bansi had no watch. He looked at the sun and said, 'It is past three. When will that ayah of yours be home? She is more frightening than your grandmother!'

'She comes at four.'

'Then we must hurry back. And don't tell her where we've been, or I'll never be able to come to your house again. Your grandmother's one of my best customers.'

'That means you'd be sorry if she died.'

'I would indeed, my friend.'

Bansi raced the tonga back to town. There was very little motor traffic in those days, and tongas and bullock-carts were far more numerous than they are today.

We were back five minutes before Ayah returned. Before Bansi left, he promised to take me for another ride the following week.

♦

The house in Dehra had to be sold. My father had not left any money; he had never realized that his health would deteriorate so rapidly from the malarial fevers which had grown in frequency; he was still planning for the future when he died. Now that my father had gone, Grandmother saw no point in staying on in India; there was nothing left in the bank and she needed money for our passages to England, so the house had to go. Dr Ghose, who had a thriving medical practice in Dehra, made her a reasonable offer, which she accepted.

Then things happened very quickly. Grandmother sold most of our belongings, because as she said, we wouldn't be able to cope with a lot of luggage. The kabaris came in droves, buying our crockery, furniture, carpets and clocks at throwaway prices. Grandmother hated parting with some of her possessions, such as the carved giltwood mirror, her walnut-wood armchair and her rosewood writing desk, but it was impossible to take them with us. They were carried away in a bullock-cart.

Ayah was very unhappy at first but cheered up when Grandmother got her a job with a tea-planter's family in Assam. It was arranged that she could stay with us until we left Dehra.

We left at the end of September, just as the monsoon clouds broke up, scattered, and were driven away by soft breezes from the Himalayas. There was no time to revisit the island where my father and I had planted our trees. And in the urgency and excitement of the preparations for our departure, I forgot to recover my small treasures from the hole in the banyan tree. It was only when we were in Bansi's tonga, on the way to the station, that I remembered my top, catapult and Iron Cross. Too late! To go back for them would mean missing the train.

'Hurry!' urged Grandmother nervously. 'We mustn't be late for the train, Bansi.'

Bansi flicked the reins and shouted to his pony, and for once in her life Grandmother submitted to being carried along the road at a brisk trot.

'It's five to nine,' she said, 'and the train leaves at nine.'

'Do not worry, Memsahib. I have been taking you to the station for fifteen years, and you have never missed a train!'

'No,' said Grandmother. 'And I don't suppose you'll ever take me to the station again, Bansi.'

'Times are changing, Memsahib. Do you know that there is now a taxi—a *motor car*—competing with the tongas of Dehra? You are lucky to be leaving. If you stay, you will see me starve to death!'

'We will all starve to death if we don't catch that train,' said Grandmother.

'Do not worry about the train, it never leaves on time, and no one expects it to. If it left at nine o' clock, everyone would miss it.'

Bansi was right. We arrived at the station at five minutes past nine, and rushed on to the platform, only to find that the train had not yet arrived.

The platform was crowded with people waiting to catch the same train or to meet people arriving on it. Ayah was there already, standing guard over a pile of miscellaneous luggage. We sat down on our boxes and became part of the platform life at an Indian railway station.

Moving among piles of bedding and luggage were sweating, cursing coolies; vendors of magazines, sweetmeats, tea and betel-leaf preparations; also stray dogs, stray people and sometimes a stray stationmaster. The cries of the vendors mixed with the general clamour of the station and the shunting of a steam engine in the yards. 'Tea, hot tea!' Sweets, papads, hot stuff, cold drinks, toothpowder, pictures of film stars, bananas, balloons, wooden toys, clay images of the gods. The platform had become a bazaar.

Ayah was giving me all sorts of warnings.

'Remember, baba, don't lean out of the window when the train is moving. There was that American boy who lost his head last year! And don't eat rubbish at every station between here and Bombay. And see that no strangers enter the compartment. Mr Wilkins was murdered *and* robbed last year!'

The station bell clanged, and in the distance there appeared a big, puffing steam engine, painted green and gold and black. A stray dog, with a lifetime's experience of trains, darted away across the railway lines. As the train came alongside the platform, doors opened, window shutters fell, faces appeared in the openings, and even before the train had come to a stop, people were trying to get in or out.

For a few moments there was chaos. The crowd surged backward and forward. No one could get out. No one could get in. A hundred people were leaving the train, two hundred were getting into it. No one wanted to give way.

The problem was solved by a man climbing out of a window. Others followed his example and the pressure at the doors eased and people started squeezing into their compartments.

Grandmother had taken the precaution of reserving berths in a first-class compartment, and assisted by Bansi and half a dozen coolies, we were soon inside with all our luggage. A whistle blasted and we were off! Bansi had to jump from the running train.

As the engine gathered speed, I ignored Ayah's advice and put my head out of the window to look back at the receding platform. Ayah and Bansi were standing on the platform, waving to me and I kept waving to them until the train rushed into the darkness and the bright lights of Dehra were swallowed up in the night. New lights, dim and flickering came into existence as we passed small villages. The stars too were visible and I saw a shooting star streaking through the heavens.

I remembered something that Ayah had once told me, that stars are the spirits of good men, and I wondered if that shooting star was a sign from my father that he was aware of our departure and would be with us on our journey. And I remembered something else that Ayah had said—that if one wished on a shooting star, one's wish would be granted, provided of course that one thrust all five fingers into the mouth at the same time!

'What on earth are you doing?' asked Grandmother staring at me as I thrust my hand into my mouth.

'Making a wish,' I said.

'Oh,' said Grandmother.

She was preoccupied, and didn't ask me what I was wishing for; nor did I tell her.

CALYPSO CHRISTMAS

My first Christmas in London had been a lonely one. My small bed-sitting-room near Swiss Cottage had been cold and austere, and my landlady had disapproved of any sort of revelry. Moreover, I hadn't the money for the theatre or a good restaurant. That first English Christmas was spent sitting in front of a lukewarm gas-fire, eating beans on toast, and drinking cheap sherry. My one consolation was the row of Christmas cards on the mantelpiece—most of them from friends in India.

But in the following year I was making more money and living in a bigger, brighter, homelier room. The new landlady approved of my bringing friends—even girls—to the house, and had even made me a plum pudding so that I could entertain my guests. My friends in London included a number of Indian and Commonwealth students, and through them I met George, a friendly, sensitive person from Trinidad.

George was not a student. He was over thirty. Like thousands of other West Indians, he had come to England because he had been told that jobs were plentiful, that there was a free health scheme and national insurance, and that he could earn anything from ten to twenty pounds a week—far more than he could make in Trinidad or Jamaica. But, while it was true that jobs were to be had in England, it was also true that sections of local labour resented outsiders filling these posts. There were also those, belonging chiefly to the lower middle-classes, who were prone to various prejudices, and though these people were a minority, they were still capable of making themselves felt and heard.

In any case, London is a lonely place, especially for the stranger. And for the happy-go-lucky West Indian, accustomed to sunshine, colour and music, London must be quite baffling.

As though to match the grey-green fogs of winter, Londoners wore sombre colours, greys and browns. The West Indians couldn't understand this. Surely, they reasoned, during a grey season the colours worn should be vivid reds and greens—colours that would defy the curling fog and uncomfortable rain? But Londoners frowned on these gay splashes of colour: to them it all seemed an expression of some sort of barbarism. And then again Londoners had a horror of any sort of loud noise, and a blaring radio could (quite justifiably) bring in scores of protests from neighbouring houses. The West Indians, on the other hand, liked letting off steam; they liked holding parties in their rooms at which there was much singing and shouting. They had always believed that England was their mother country, and so, despite rain, fog, sleet and snow, they were determined to live as they had lived back home in Trinidad. And it is to their credit, and even to the credit of indigenous Londoners, that this is what they succeeded in doing.

George worked for the British Railways. He was a ticket

collector at one of the underground stations; he liked his work, and received about ten pounds a week for collecting tickets. A large, stout man, with huge hands and feet, he always had a gentle, kindly expression on his mobile face. Amongst other accomplishments he could play the piano, and as there was an old, rather dilapidated piano in my room, he would often come over in the evenings to run his fat, heavy fingers over the keys, playing tunes that ranged from hymns to jazz pieces. I thought he would be a nice person to spend Christmas with, so I asked him to come and share the pudding my landlady had made, and a bottle of sherry I had procured.

Little did I realize that an invitation to George would he interpreted as an invitation to all of George's friends and relations—in fact, anyone who had known him in Trinidad—but this was the way he looked at it, and at eight o' clock on Christmas Eve, while a chilly wind blew dead leaves down from Hampstead Heath, I saw a veritable army of West Indians marching down Belsize Avenue, with George in the lead.

Bewildered, I opened my door to them; and in streamed George, George's cousins, George's nephews and George's friends. They were all smiling and shaking hands with me, making complimentary remarks about my room ('Man, that's some piano!' 'Hey, look at that crazy picture!' 'This rocking chair gives me fever!') and took no time at all to feel and make themselves at home. Everyone had brought something along for the party. George had brought several bottles of beer. Eric, a flashy, coffee-coloured youth, had brought cigarettes and more beer. Marian, a buxom woman of thirty-five, who called me 'darling' as soon as we met, and kissed me on the cheeks saying she adored pink cheeks, had brought bacon and eggs. Her daughter Lucy, who was sixteen and in the full bloom of youth, had brought a gramophone, while the little nephews carried the records. Other friends and familiars had also brought beer; and one enterprising fellow produced a bottle of Jamaican rum.

Then everything began to happen at once.

Lucy put a record on the gramophone, and the strains of 'Basin Street Blues' filled the room. At the same time George sat down at the piano to hammer out an accompaniment to the record: his huge hands crushed down on the keys as though he were chopping up chunks of meat. Marian had lit the gas-fire and was busy frying bacon and eggs. Eric was opening beer bottles. In the midst of the noise and confusion I heard a knock on the door—a very timid, hesitant sort of knock—and opening it, found my landlady standing on the threshold.

'Oh, Mr Bond, the neighbours—' she began; and glancing into the room was rendered speechless.

'It's only tonight,' I said. 'They'll all go home after an hour. Remember, it's Christmas!'

She nodded mutely and hurried away down the corridor, pursued by something called 'Be-Bop-A-Lola'. I closed the door and drew all the curtains in an effort to stifle the noise; but everyone was stamping about on the floorboards, and I hoped fervently that the downstairs people had gone to the theatre. George had started playing calypso music, and Eric and Lucy were strutting and stomping in the middle of the room, while the two nephews were improvising on their own. Before I knew what was happening, Marian had taken me in her strong arms, and was teaching me to do the calypso. The song playing, I think, was 'Banana Boat Song'.

Instead of the party lasting an hour, it lasted three hours. We ate innumerable fried eggs and finished off all the beer. I took turns dancing with Marian, Lucy and the nephews. There was a peculiar expression they used when excited. 'Fire!' they shouted. I never knew what was supposed to be on fire, or what the exclamation implied, but I too shouted 'Fire!' and somehow it seemed a very sensible thing to shout.

Perhaps their hearts were on fire, I don't know; but for all their excitability and flashiness and brashness they were lovable and sincere friends, and today, when I look back on my two years in London, that Christmas party is the brightest, most vivid memory of all, and the faces of George and Marian, Lucy and Eric, are the faces I remember best.

At midnight someone turned out the light. I was dancing with Lucy at the time, and in the dark she threw her arms around me and kissed me full on the lips. It was the first time I had been kissed by a girl, and when I think about it, I am glad that it was Lucy who kissed me.

When they left, they went in a bunch, just as they had come. I stood at the gate and watched them saunter down the dark, empty street. The buses and tubes had stopped running at midnight, and George and his friends would have to walk all the way back to their rooms at Highgate and Golders Green.

After they had gone, the street was suddenly empty and silent, and my own footsteps were the only sounds I could hear. The cold came clutching at me, and I turned up my collar. I looked up at the windows of my house, and at the windows of all the other houses in the street. They were all in darkness. It seemed to me that we were the only ones who had really celebrated Christmas.

SITA AND THE RIVER

The Island in the River

In the middle of the river, the river that began in the mountains of the Himalayas and ended in the Bay of Bengal, there was a small island. The river swept round the island, sometimes clawing at its banks but never going right over it. The river was still deep and swift at this point, because the foothills were only forty miles distant. More than twenty years had passed since the river had flooded the island, and at that time no one had lived there. But ten years ago a small family had came to live on the island, and now a small hut stood on it, mud-walled hut with a sloping thatched roof. The hut had been built into a huge rock. Only three of its walls were mud, the fourth was rock.

A few goats grazed on the short grass and the prickly leaves of the thistle. Some hens followed them about. There was a melon patch and a vegetable patch and a small field of marigolds. The marigolds were sometimes made into garlands, and the garlands were sold during weddings or festivals in the nearby town.

In the middle of the islands stood a peepul tree. It was the only tree on this tongue of land. But peepul trees will grow anywhere—through the walls of old temples, through gravestones, even from rooftops. It is usually the buildings, and not the trees, that give way!

Even during the great flood, which had occurred twenty years back, the peepul tree had stood firm.

It was an old tree, much older than the old man on the island, who was only seventy. The peepul was about three hundred. It also provided shelter for the birds who sometimes visited it from the mainland.

Three hundred years ago, the land on which the peepul tree stood had been part of the mainland; but the river had changed its course, and that bit of land with the tree on it had become an island. The tree had lived alone for many years. Now it gave shade and shelter to a small family, who were grateful for its presence.

The people of India love peepul trees, especially during the hot summer months when the heart-shaped leaves catch the least breath of air and flutter eagerly, fanning those who sit beneath.

A sacred tree, the peepul, the abode of spirits, good and bad.

'Do not yawn when you are sitting beneath the tree,' Grandmother would warn Sita, her ten-year-old granddaughter. 'And if you must yawn always snap your fingers in front of your mouth. If you forget to do that, a demon might jump down your throat!'

'And then what will happen?' asked Sita.

'He will probably ruin your digestion,' said Grandfather, who didn't take demons very seriously.

The peepul had beautiful leaves, and Grandmother likened it to the body of the mighty Lord Krishna—broad at the shoulders, then tapering down to a very slim waist.

The tree attracted birds and insects from across the river. On some nights it was full of fireflies.

Whenever Grandmother saw the fireflies, she told her favourite story.

'When we first came here,' she said, 'we were greatly troubled by mosquitoes. One night your grandfather rolled himself up in his sheet so that they couldn't get at him. After a while he peeped out of his bedsheet to make sure they were gone. He saw a firefly and said, "You clever mosquito! You could not see in the dark, so you got a lantern!"'

Grandfather was mending a fishing-net. He had fished in the river for ten years, and he was a good fisherman. He knew where to find the slim silver chilwa and the big, beautiful masheer and the singhara with its long whiskers; he knew where the river was deep and where it was shallow; he knew which baits to use—when to use worms and when to use gram. He had taught his son to fish, but his son had gone to work in a factory in a city, nearly a hundred miles away. He had no grandson; but he had a granddaughter, Sita, and she could do all the things a boy could do, and sometimes she could do them better. She had lost her mother when she was two or three. Grandmother had taught her all that a girl should know—cooking, sewing, grinding spices, cleaning the house, feeding the birds—and Grandfather had taught her other things like taking a small boat across the river, cleaning a fish, repairing a net, or catching a snake by the tail! And some things she had learnt by herself—like climbing the peepul tree, or leaping from rock to rock in shallow water, or swimming in an inlet where the water was calm.

Neither grandparent could read or write, and as a result Sita couldn't read or write.

There was a school in one of the villages across the river, but Sita had never seen it. She had never been further than Shahganj, the small market town near the river. She had never seen a city. She had never been on a train. The river cut her off from many things; but she could not miss what she had never known, and besides, she was much too busy.

While Grandfather mended his net, Sita was inside the hut, pressing her grandmother's forehead which was hot with fever. Grandmother had been ill for three days and could not eat. She had been ill before, but she had never been so bad. Grandfather had brought her some sweet oranges from Shahganj, and she could suck the juice from the oranges, but she couldn't take anything else.

She was younger than Grandfather, but, because she was sick, she looked much older. She had never been very strong. She coughed a lot, and sometimes she had difficulty in breathing.

When Sita noticed that Grandmother was sleeping, she left the bedside and tiptoed out of the room on her bare feet.

Outside, she found the sky dark with monsoon clouds. It had rained all night, and, in a few hours, it would rain again. The monsoon rains had come early, at the end of June. Now it was the end of July, and already the river was swollen. Its rushing sound seemed nearer and more menacing than usual.

Sita went to her grandfather and sat down beside him.

'When you are hungry, tell me,' she said, 'and I will make the bread.'

'Is your Grandmother asleep?'

'Yes. But she will wake soon. The pain is deep.'

The old man stared out across the river, at the dark green of the forest, at the leaden sky, and said, 'If she is not better by morning, I will take her to the hospital in Shahganj. They will know how to make her well. You may be on your own for two or three days. You have been on your own before.'

Sita nodded gravely—she had been alone before; but not in the middle of the rains, with the river so high. But she knew that someone must stay behind. She wanted Grandmother to get well, and she knew that only Grandfather could take the small boat across the river when the current was so strong.

Sita was not afraid of being left alone, but she did not like the look of the river. That morning, when she had been fetching water, she had noticed that the lever suddenly disappeared.

'Grandfather, if the river rises higher, what will I do?'

'You must keep to the high ground.'

'And if the water reaches the high ground?'

'Then go into the hut, and take the hens with you.'

'And if the water comes into the hut?'

'Then climb into the peepul tree. It is a strong tree. It will not fall. And the water cannot rise higher than the tree.'

'And the goats, Grandfather?'

'I will be taking them with me. I may have to sell them, to pay for good food and medicines for your Grandmother. As for the hens, you can put them on the roof if the water enters the hut. But do not worry too much'—and he patted Sita's head—'the water will not rise so high. Has it ever done so? I will be back soon, remember that.'

'And won't Grandmother come back?'

'Yes—but they may keep her in the hospital for some time.'

The Sound of the River

That evening it began to rain again. Big pellets of rain, scarring the surface of the river. But it was warm rain, and Sita could move about in it. She was not afraid of getting wet, she rather liked it. In the previous month, when the first monsoon shower had arrived, washing the dusty leaves of the tree and bringing up the good smell of the earth, she had exulted in it, had run about shouting for joy. She was used to it now, even a little tired of the rain, but she did not mind getting wet. It was steamy indoors, and her thin dress would soon dry in the heat from the kitchen fire.

She walked about barefooted, barelegged. She was very sure on her feet; her toes had grown accustomed to gripping all kinds of rocks, slippery or sharp. And though thin, she was surprisingly strong.

Black hair, streaming across her face. Black eyes. Slim brown arms. A scar on her thigh: when she was small, visiting her mother's village, a hyaena had entered the house where she was sleeping, fastened on to her leg and tried to drag her away; but her screams had roused the villagers, and the hyaena had run off.

She moved about in the pouring rain, chasing the hens into a shelter behind the hut. A harmless brown snake, flooded out of its hole, was moving across the open ground. Sita took a stick, picked the snake up with it, and dropped it behind a cluster of rocks. She had no quarrel with snakes. They kept down the rats and the frogs. She wondered how the rats had first come to the island—probably in someone's boat or in a sack of grain.

She disliked the huge black scorpions who left their waterlogged dwellings and tried to take shelter in the hut. It was so easy to step on one, and the sting could be very painful. She had been bitten by a scorpion the previous monsoon, and for a day and a night she had known fever and great pain. Sita had never killed living creatures, but now, whenever she found a scorpion, she crushed it with a rock!

When, finally, she went indoors, she was hungry. She ate some parched gram and warmed up some goat's milk.

Grandmother woke once, and asked for water, and Grandfather held the brass tumbler to her lips.

It rained all night.

The roof was leaking, and a small puddle formed on the floor. Grandfather kept the kerosene-lamps alight. They did not need the light but somehow it made them feel safer.

The sound of the river had always been with them, although they seldom noticed it; but that night they noticed a change in its sound. There was something like a moan, like a wind in the tops of tall trees, and a swift hiss as the water swept round the rocks and carried away pebbles. And sometimes there was a rumble, as loose earth fell into the water. Sita could not sleep.

She had a rag doll, made with Grandmother's help out of bits of old clothing. She kept it by her side every night.

The doll was someone to talk to, when the nights were long and sleep elusive. Her grandparents were often ready to talk; but sometimes Sita wanted to have secrets, and, though there were no special secrets in her life, she made up a few because it was fun to have them. And if you have secrets, you must have a friend to share them with. Since there were no other children on the island, Sita shared her secrets with the rag doll, whose name was Mumta.

Grandfather and Grandmother were asleep, though the sound of Grandmother's laboured breathing was almost as persistent as the sound of the river.

'Mumta,' whispered Sita in the dark, starting one of her private conversations.

'Do you think Grandmother will get well again?'

Mumta always answered Sita's questions, even though the answers were really Sita's answers.

'She is very old,' said Mumta.

'Do you think the river will reach the hut?' asked Sita.

'If it keeps raining like this, and the river keeps rising, it will reach the hut.'

'I am afraid of the river, Mumta. Aren't you afraid?'

'Don't be afraid. The river has always been good to us.'

'What will we do if it comes into the hut?'

'We will climb on the roof.'

'And if it reaches the roof?'

'We will climb the peepul tree. The river has never gone higher than the peepul tree.'

As soon as the first light showed through the little skylight, Sita got up and went outside. It wasn't raining hard, it was drizzling, but it was the sort of drizzle that could continue for days, and it probably meant that heavy rain was falling in the hills where the river began.

Sita went down to the water's edge. She couldn't find her favourite rock, the one on which she often sat dangling her feet in the water, watching the little chilwa fish swim by. It was still there, no doubt, but the river had gone over it.

She stood on the sand, and she could feel the water oozing and bubbling beneath her feet.

The river was no longer green and blue and flecked with white; it was a muddy colour.

She went back to the hut. Grandfather was up now. He was getting his boat ready.

Sita milked the goat, thinking that perhaps it was the last time she would be milking it; but she did not care for the goat in the same way that she cared for Mumta.

The sun was just coming up when Grandfather pushed off in the boat. Grandmother lay in the prow. She was staring hard at Sita, trying to speak, but the words would not come. She raised her hand in a blessing.

Sita bent and touched her Grandmother's feet, and then Grandfather pushed off. The little boat—with its two old people and three goats—rode swiftly on the river, edging its way towards the opposite bank. The current was very swift, and the boat would be carried about half a mile downstream before Grandfather would be able to get it to dry land.

It bobbed about on the water, getting smaller and smaller, until it was just a speck on the broad river.

And suddenly Sita was alone.

There was a wind, whipping the raindrops against her face; and there was the water, rushing past the island; and there was the distant shore, blurred by rain; and there was the small hut; and there was the tree.

Sita got busy. The hens had to be fed. They weren't concerned about anything except food. Sita threw them handfuls of coarse grain, potato-peels and peanut shells.

Then she took the broom and swept out the hut; lit the charcoal-burner, warmed some milk, and thought, 'Tomorrow there will be no milk...' She began peeling onions. Soon her eyes started smarting, and, pausing for a few moments and glancing round the quiet room, she became aware again that she was alone. Grandfather's hookah pipe stood by itself in one corner. It was a beautiful old hookah, which had belonged to Sita's great-grandfather. The bowl was made out of a coconut encased in silver. The long winding stem was at least four feet long. It was their most treasured possession. Grandmother's sturdy shisham-wood walking stick stood in another corner.

Sita looked around for Mumta, found the doll beneath the light wooden charpoy, and placed her within sight and hearing.

Thunder rolled down from the hills. Boom—boom—boom...

'The gods of the mountains are angry,' said Sita. 'Do you think they are angry with me?'

'Why should they be angry with you?' asked Mumta.

'They don't need a reason for being angry. They are angry with everything, and we are in the middle of everything. We are so small—do you think they know we are here?'

'Who knows what the gods think?'

'But I made you,' said Sita, 'and I know you are here.'

'And will you save me if the river rises?'

'Yes, of course. I won't go anywhere without you, Mumta.'

The Water Rises

Sita couldn't stay indoors for long. She went out, taking Mumta with her, and stared out across the river, to the safe land on the other side. But was it really safe there? The river looked much wider now. It had crept over its banks and spread far across the flat plain. Far away, people were driving their cattle through waterlogged, flooded fields, carrying their belongings in bundles on their heads or shoulders, leaving their homes, making for high land. It wasn't safe anywhere.

Sita wondered what had happened to Grandfather and Grandmother. If they had reached the shore safely, Grandfather would have to engage a bullock-cart or a pony-drawn carriage to get Grandmother to the district hospital, five or six miles away. Shahganj had a market, a court, a jail, a cinema and a hospital.

She wondered if she would ever see Grandmother again. She had done her best to look after the old lady, remembering the times when Grandmother had looked after her, had gently touched her fevered brow, and had told her stories—stories about the gods—about the young Krishna, friend of birds and animals, so full of mischief, always causing confusion among the other gods. He made Lord Indra angry by shifting a mountain without permission. Indra was the God of the clouds, who made the thunder and lightning, and when he was angry he sent down a deluge such as this one.

The island looked much smaller now. Some of its mud banks had dissolved quickly, sinking into the river. But in the middle of the island there was rocky ground, and the rocks would never crumble, they could only be submerged.

Sita climbed into the tree to get a better view of the flood. She had climbed the tree many times, and it took her only a few seconds to reach the higher branches. She put her hand to her eyes as a shield from the rain, and gazed upstream.

There was water everywhere. The world had become one vast river. Even the trees on the forested side of the river looked as though they had grown from the water, like mangroves. The sky was banked with massive, moisture-laden clouds. Thunder rolled down from the hills, and the river seemed to take it up with a hollow booming sound.

Something was floating down the river, something big and bloated. It was closer now, and Sita could make out its bulk—a drowned bullock, being carried downstream.

So the water had already flooded the villages further upstream. Or perhaps the bullock had strayed too close to the rising river.

Sita's worst fears were confirmed when, a little later, she saw planks of wood, small trees and bushes, and then a wooden bedstead, floating past the island.

As she climbed down from the tree, it began to rain more heavily. She ran indoors, shooing the hens before her. They flew into the hut and huddled under Grandmother's cot. Sita thought it would be best to keep them together now.

There were three hens and a cockbird. The river did not bother them. They were interested only in food, and Sita kept them content by throwing them a handful of onion-skins.

She would have liked to close the door and shut out the swish of the rain and the boom of the river; but then she would have no way of knowing how fast the water rose.

She took Mumta in her arms and began praying for the

rain to stop and the river to fall. She prayed to Lord Indra, and, just in case he was busy elsewhere, she prayed to other gods too. She prayed for the safety of her grandparents and for her own safety. She put herself last—but only after an effort!

Finally Sita decided to make herself a meal. So she chopped up some onions, fried them, then added turmeric and red chilli powder, salt and water, and stirred until she had everything sizzling; and then she added a cup of lentils and covered the pot.

Doing this took her about ten minutes. It would take about half an hour for the dish to cook.

When she looked outside, she saw pools of water among the rocks. She couldn't tell if it was rainwater or overflow from the river.

She had an idea.

A big tin trunk stood in a corner of the room. In it Grandmother kept an old single-thread sewing-machine. It had belonged once to an English lady, had found its way to a Shahganj junkyard, and had been rescued by Grandfather who had paid fifteen rupees for it. It was just over a hundred years old, but it could still be used.

The trunk also contained an old sword. This had originally belonged to Sita's great-grandfather, who had used it to help defend his village against marauding Rohilla soldiers more than a century ago. Sita could tell that it had been used to fight with, because there were several small dents in the steel blade.

But there was no time for Sita to start admiring family heirlooms. She decided to stuff the trunk with everything useful or valuable. There was a chance that it wouldn't be carried away by the water.

Grandfather's hookah went into the trunk. Grandmother's

walking stick went in, too. So did a number of small tins containing the spices used in cooking—nutmeg, caraway seeds, cinnamon, corrainder, pepper—also a big tin of flour and another of molasses. Even if she had to spend several hours in the tree, there would be something to eat when she came down again.

A clean white cotton dhoti of Grandfather's, and Grandmother's only spare sari also went into the trunk. Never mind if they got stained with curry powder! Never mind if they got the smell of salted fish—some of that went in, too.

Sita was so busy packing the trunk that she paid no attention to the lick of cold water at her heels. She locked the trunk, dropped the key into a crack in the rock wall, and turned to give her attention to the food. It was only then that she discovered that she was walking about on a watery floor.

She stood still, horrified by what she saw. The water was oozing over the doorsill, pushing its way into the room.

In her fright, Sita forgot about her meal and everything else. Darting out of the hut, she ran splashing through ankle-deep water toward the safety of the peepul tree. If the tree hadn't been there, such a well-known landmark, she might have floundered into deep water, into the river.

She climbed swiftly into the strong arms of the tree, made herself comfortable on a familiar branch, and pushed the wet hair away from her eyes.

The Tree

She was glad she had hurried. The hut was now surrounded by water. Only the higher parts of the island could still be seen—a few rocks, the big rock into which the hut was built, a hillock on which some brambles and thorn-apples grew.

The hens hadn't bothered to leave the hut. Instead, they were perched on the wooden bedstead.

'Will the river rise still higher?' wondered Sita. She had never seen it like this before. With a deep, muffled roar it swirled around her, stretching away in all directions.

The most unusual things went by on the water—an aluminium kettle, a cane chair, a tin of tooth powder, an empty cigarette packet, a wooden slipper, a plastic doll...

A doll!

With a sinking feeling, Sita remembered Mumta.

Poor Mumta, she had been left behind in the hut. Sita, in her hurry, had forgotten her only companion.

She climbed down from the tree and ran splashing through the water towards the hut. Already the current was pulling at her legs. When she reached the hut, she found it full of water. The hens had gone—and so had Mumta.

Sita struggled back to the tree. She was only just in time, for the waters were higher now, the island fast disappearing.

She crouched miserably in the fork of the tree, watching her world disappear. She had always loved the river. Why was it threatening her now? She remembered the doll, and she thought, 'If I can be so careless with someone I have made, how can I expect the gods to notice me?'

Something went floating past the tree. Sita caught a glimpse of a stiff, upraised arm and long hair streaming behind on the water. The body of a drowned woman. It was soon gone, but it made Sita feel very small and lonely, at the mercy of great and cruel forces. She began to shiver and then to cry.

She stopped crying when she saw an empty kerosene tin, with one of the hens perched on top. The tin came bobbing along on the water and sailed slowly past the tree. The hen looked a bit ruffled but seemed secure on its perch.

A little later Sita saw the remaining hens fly up to the rock ledge to huddle there in a small recess.

The water was still rising. All that remained of the island was the big rock behind the hut, and the top of the hut, and the peepul tree.

She climbed a little higher, into the crook of a branch. A jungle crow settled in the branches above her. Sita saw the nest, the crow's nest, an untidy platform of twigs wedged in the fork of a branch.

In the nest were four speckled eggs. The crow sat on them and cawed disconsolately. But though the bird sounded miserable its presence brought some cheer to Sita. At least she was not alone. Better to have a crow for company than no one at all.

Other things came floating out of the hut—a large pumpkin; a red turban belonging to Grandfather, unwinding in the water like a long snake; and then—Mumta!

The doll, being filled with straw and wood shavings moved quite swiftly on the water, too swiftly for Sita to do anything about rescuing it. Sita wanted to call out, to urge her friend to make for the tree; but she knew that Mumta could not swim—the doll could only float, travel with the river, and perhaps be washed ashore many miles downstream.

The trees shook in the wind and the rain. The crow cawed and flew up, circled the tree a few times, then returned to the nest. Sita clung to the branch.

The tree trembled throughout its tall frame. To Sita it felt like an earthquake tremor; she felt the shudder of the tree in her own bones.

The river swirled all around her now. It was almost up to the roof of the hut. Soon the mud walls would crumble and vanish. Except for the big rock and some trees very far away, there was only water to be seen. Water, and grey weeping sky.

In the distance, a boat with several people in it moved sluggishly away from the ruins of a flooded village. Someone looked out across the flooded river and said, 'See, there is a tree right in the middle of the river! How could it have got there? Isn't someone moving the tree?'

But the others thought he was imagining things it was only a tree carried down by the flood, they said. In worrying about their own distress, they had forgotten about the island in the middle of the river.

The river was very angry now, rampaging down from the hills and thundering across the plain, bringing with it dead animals, uprooted trees, household goods and huge fishes choked to death by the swirling mud.

The peepul tree groaned. Its long, winding roots still clung tenaciously to the earth from which it had sprung many, many years ago. But the earth was softening, the stones were being washed away. The roots of the tree were rapidly losing their hold.

The crow must have known that something was wrong because it kept flying up and circling the tree, reluctant to settle in it, yet unwilling to fly away. As long as the nest was there, the crow would remain too.

Sita's wet cotton dress clung to her thin body. The rain

streamed down from her long black hair. It poured from every leaf of the tree. The crow, too, was drenched and groggy.

The tree groaned and moved again.

There was a flurry of leaves, then a surge of mud from below. To Sita it seemed as though the river was rising to meet the sky. The tree tilted swinging Sita from side to side. Her feet were in the water but she clung tenaciously to her branch.

And then, she found the tree moving, moving with the river, rocking her about, dragging its roots along the ground as it set out on the first and last journey of its life.

And as the tree moved out on the river and the little island was lost in the swirling waters, Sita forgot her fear and her loneliness. The tree was taking her with it. She was not alone. It was as though one of the gods had remembered her after all.

Taken with the Flood

The branches swung Sita about, but she did not lose her grip. The tree was her friend. It had known her all these years, and now it held her in its old and dying arms as though it were determined to keep her from the river.

The crow kept flying around the moving tree. The bird was in a great rage. Its nest was still up there—but not for long! The tree lurched and twisted, and the nest fell into the water. Sita saw the eggs sink.

The crow swooped low over the water but there was nothing it could do. In a few moments the nest had disappeared.

The bird followed the tree for some time; then, flapping its wings, it rose high into the air and flew across the river until it was out of sight.

Sita was alone once more. But there was no time for feeling lonely. Everything was in motion—up and down and sideways and forwards.

She saw a turtle swimming past—a great big river turtle, the kind that feeds on decaying flesh. Sita turned her face away. In the distance she saw a flooded village and people in flat-bottomed boats; but they were very far.

Because of its great size, the tree did not move very swiftly on the river. Sometimes, when it reached shallow water, it stopped, its roots catching in the rocks; but not for long: the river's momentum soon swept it on.

At one place, where there was a bend in the river, the tree struck a sandbank and was still. It would not move again.

Sita felt very tired. Her arms were aching and she had to cling tightly to her branch to avoid slipping into the water. The rain blurred her vision. She wondered if she should brave the current and try swimming to safety. But she did not want to leave the tree. It was all that was left to her now, and she felt safe in its branches.

Then, above the sound of the river, she heard someone calling. The voice was faint and seemed very far but, looking upriver through the curtain of rain, Sita was able to make out a small boat coming towards her.

There was a boy in the boat. He seemed quite at home in the turbulent river, and he was smiling at Sita as he guided his boat towards the tree. He held on to one of the branches to steady himself, and gave his free hand to Sita.

She grasped the outstretched hand and slipped into the boat beside the boy. He placed his bare foot against the trunk of the tree and pushed away.

The little boat moved swiftly down the river. Sita looked back and saw the big tree lying on its side on the sandbank, while the river swirled round it and pulled at its branches, carrying away its beautiful slender leaves.

And then the tree grew smaller and was left far behind. A new journey had begun.

The Boy in the Boat

She lay stretched out in the boat, too tired to talk, too tired to move. The boy looked at her but he did not say anything, he just kept smiling. He leaned on his two small oars, stroking smoothly, rhythmically, trying to keep from going into the middle of the river. He wasn't strong enough to get the boat right out of the swift current; but he kept trying.

A small boat on a big river—a river that had broken its bounds and reached across the plains in every direction—the boat moved swiftly on the wild brown water, and the girl's home and the boy's home were both left far behind.

The boy wore only a loincloth. He was a slim, wiry boy, with a hard flat belly. He had high cheekbones, strong white teeth. He was a little darker than Sita.

He did not speak until they reached a broader, smoother stretch of river, and then, resting on his oars and allowing the boat to drift a little, he said, 'You live on the island. I have seen you sometimes, from my boat. But where are the others?'

'My grandmother was sick,' said Sita. 'Grandfather took her to the hospital in Shahganj.'

'When did they leave?'

'Early this morning.'

Early that morning—and already Sita felt as though it had been many mornings ago!

'Where are you from?' she asked.

'I am from a village near the foothills. About six miles from your home. I was in my boat, trying to get across the river with the news that our village was badly flooded. The current was too strong. I was swept down and past your island. We cannot fight the river when it is like this, we must go where it takes us.'

'You must be tired,' said Sita. 'Give me the oars.'

'No. There is not much to do now. The river has gone wherever it wanted to go—it will not drive us before it any more.'

He brought in one oar, and with his free hand felt under the seat, where there was a small basket. He produced two mangoes, and gave one to Sita.

'I was supposed to sell these in Shahganj,' he said. 'My father is very strict. Even if I return home safely, he will ask me what I got for the mangoes!'

'And what will you tell him?'

'I will say they are at the bottom of the river!'

They bit deep into the ripe fleshy mangoes, using their teeth to tear the skin away. The sweet juice trickled down their skins. The good smell—like the smell of the leaves of the cosmos flower when crushed between the palms—helped to revive Sita. The flavour of the fruit was heavenly—truly the nectar of the gods!

Sita hadn't tasted a mango for over a year. For a few moments she forgot about everything else. All that mattered was the sweet, dizzy flavour of the mango.

The boat drifted, but slowly now, for as they went further downstream, the river gradually lost its power and fury. It was late afternoon when the rain stopped; but the clouds did not break up.

'My father has many buffaloes,' said the boy, 'but several have been lost in the flood.'

'Do you go to school?' asked Sita.

'Yes, I am supposed to go to school. I don't always go, at least, not when the weather is fine! There is a school near our village. I don't think you go to school?'

'No. There is too much work at home.'

'Can you read and write?'

'Only a little...'

'Then you should go to a school.'

'It is too far away.'

'True. But you should know how to read and write. Otherwise you will be stuck on your island for the rest of your life—that is, if your island is still there!'

'But I like the island,' protested Sita.

'Because you are with people you love,' said the boy. 'But your grandparents, they are old, they will die some day—and then you will be alone, and will you like the island then?'

Sita did not answer. She was trying to think of what life would be like without her grandparents. It would be an empty island, that was true. She would be imprisoned by the river.

'I can help you,' said the boy. 'When we get back—if we get back—I will come to see you sometimes, and I will teach you to read and write. All right?'

'Yes,' said Sita, nodding thoughtfully. 'When we get back...'

The boy smiled.

'My name is Krishan,' he said.

Towards evening the river changed colour. The sun, low in the sky, broke through a rift in the clouds, and the river changed slowly from grey to gold, from gold to a deep orange, and then, as the sun went down, all these colours were drowned in the river, and the river took the colour of the night.

The moon was almost at the full, and they could see a belt of forest along the line of the river.

'I will try to reach the trees,' said Krishan.

He pulled for the trees, and after ten minutes of strenuous rowing reached a bend in the river and was able to escape the pull of the main current.

Soon they were in a forest, rowing between tall trees, sal and shisham.

The boat moved slowly as Krishan took it in and out of the trees, while the moonlight made a crooked silver path over the water.

'We will tie the boat to a tree,' he said. 'Then we can rest. Tomorrow, we will have to find out a way out of the forest.'

He produced a length of rope from the bottom of the boat, tied one end to the boat's stern, and threw the other end over a stout branch which hung only a few feet above the water. The boat came to rest against the trunk of the tree.

It was a tall, sturdy tree, the Indian mahogany. It was a safe place, for there was no rush of water in the forest; and the trees grew close together, making the earth firm and unyielding.

But those who lived in the forest were on the move. The animals had been flooded out of their holes, caves and lairs, and were looking for shelter and high ground.

Sita and Krishan had just finished tying the boat to the

tree when they saw a huge python gliding over the water towards them.

'Do you think it will try to get into the boat?' asked Sita.

'I don't think so,' said Krishan, although he took the precaution of holding an oar ready to fend off the snake.

But the python went past them, its head above water, its great length trailing behind, until it was lost in the shadows.

Krishan had more mangoes in the basket, and he and Sita sucked hungrily at them while they sat in the boat.

A big sambhur-stag came threshing through the water. He did not have to swim: he was so tall that his head and shoulders remained well above the water. His antlers were big and beautiful.

'There will be other animals,' said Sita. 'Should we climb onto the tree?'

'We are quite safe in the boat,' said Krishan. 'The animals will not be dangerous tonight. They will not even hunt each other, they are only interested in reaching dry land. For once, the deer are safe from the tiger and the leopard. You lie down and sleep, I will keep watch.'

Sita stretched herself out in the boat and closed her eyes. She was very tired, and the sound of the water lapping against the sides of the boat soon lulled her to sleep.

She woke once, when a strange bird called overhead. She raised herself on one elbow; but Krishan was awake, sitting beside her, his legs drawn up and his chin resting on his knees. He was gazing out across the water. He looked blue in the moonlight, the colour of the young Lord Krishna, and for a few moments Sita was confused and wondered if the boy was actually Krishna; but when she thought about it, she decided that it wasn't possible, he was just a village boy and she had seen hundreds like him—well, not exactly like him; he was a little different...

And when she slept again, she dreamt that the boy and Krishna were one, and that she was sitting beside him on a great white bird, which flew over the mountains, over the snow peaks of the Himalayas, into the cloud-land of the gods. And there was a great rumbling sound, as though the gods were angry about the whole thing, and she woke up to this terrible sound and looked about her, and there in the moonlit glade, up to his belly in water, stood a young elephant, his trunk raised as he trumpeted his predicament to the forest—for he was a young elephant, and he was lost, and was looking for his mother.

He trumpeted again, then lowered his head and listened. And presently, from far away, came the shrill trumpeting of another elephant. It must have been the young one's mother, because he gave several excited trumpet calls, and then went stamping and churning through the floodwater towards a gap in the trees. The boat rocked in the waves made by his passing.

'It is all right,' said Krishan. 'You can go to sleep again.'
'I don't think I will sleep now,' said Sita.
'Then I will play my flute for you and the time will pass quickly.'

He produced a flute from under the seat, and putting it to his lips he began to play. And the sweetest music that Sita had ever heard came pouring from the little flute, and it seemed to fill the forest with its beautiful sound. And the music carried her away again, into the land of dreams, and they were riding on the bird once more, Sita and the blue

God, and they were passing through cloud and mist, until suddenly the sun shot through the clouds. And at that moment Sita opened her eyes and saw the sky through the branches of the mahogany tree, the shiny green leaves making a bold pattern against the blinding blue of an open sky.

The forest was drenched with sunshine. Clouds were gathering again, but for an hour or two there would be hot sun on a steamy river.

Krishan was fast asleep in the bottom of the boat. His flute lay in the palm of his half-open hand. The sun came slating across his bare brown legs. A leaf had fallen on his face, but it had not woken him, it lay on his cheek as though it had grown there.

Sita did not move about, as she did not want to wake the boy. Instead she looked around her, and she thought the water level had fallen in the night, but she couldn't be sure.

Krishan woke at last. He yawned, stretched his limbs, and sat up beside Sita.

'I am hungry,' he said.

'So am I,' said Sita.

'The last mangoes,' he said, emptying the basket of its last two mangoes.

After they had finished the fruit, they sucked the big seeds until they were quite dry. The discarded seeds floated well on the water. Sita had always preferred them to paper boats.

'We had better move on,' said Krishan.

He rowed the boat through the trees, and then for about an hour they were passing through the flooded forest, under the dripping branches of rain-washed trees. Sometimes they had to use the oars to push away vines and creepers. Sometimes submerged bushes hampered them. But they were out of the forest before ten o' clock.

The water was no longer very deep, and they were soon gliding over flooded fields. In the distance they saw a village standing on high ground. In the old days, people had built their villages on hilltops as a better defence against bandits and the soldiers of invading armies. This was an old village; and, though its inhabitants had long ago exchanged their swords for pruning forks, the hill on which it stood gave it protection from the floodwaters.

A Bullock-Cart Ride

The people of the village were at first reluctant to help Sita and Krishan.

'They are strangers,' said an old woman. 'They are not our people.'

'They are of low caste,' said another. 'They cannot remain with us.'

'Nonsense!' said a tall, turbaned farmer, twirling his long white moustache. 'They are children, not robbers. They will come into my house.'

The people of the village—long-limbed, sturdy men and women of the Jat caste—were generous by nature, and once the elderly farmer had given them the lead they were friendly and helpful.

Sita was anxious to get to her grandparents; and the farmer, who had business to transact at a village fair some twenty miles distant, offered to take Sita and Krishan with him.

The fair was being held at a place called Karauli, and

at Karauli there was a railway station, and a train went to Shahganj.

It was a journey that Sita would always remember. The bullock-cart was so slow on the waterlogged roads that there was plenty of time in which to see things, to notice one another, to talk, to think, to dream.

Krishan couldn't sit still in the cart. He was used to the swift, gliding movements of his boat (which he had had to leave behind in the village), and every now and then he would jump off the cart and walk beside it, often ankle-deep in water.

There were four of them in the cart. Sita and Krishan, Hukam Singh, the Jat farmer; and his son, Phambiri, a mountain of a man who was going to take part in the wrestling matches at the fair.

Hukam Singh, who drove the bullocks, liked to talk. He had been a soldier in the British Indian Army during the First World War, and had been with his regiment to Italy and Mesopotamia.

'There is nothing to compare with soldiering,' he said, 'except, of course, farming. If you can't be a farmer, be a soldier. Are you listening, boy? Which will you be—farmer or soldier?'

'Neither,' said Krishan. 'I shall be an engineer!'

Hukam Singh's long moustaches seemed to almost bristle with indignation.

'An engineer! What next! What does your father do, boy?'

'He keeps buffaloes.'

'Ah! And his son would be an engineer?... Well, well, the world isn't what it used to be! No one knows his rightful place any more. Men sent their children to schools, and what is the result? Engineers! And who will look after the buffaloes, while you are engineering?'

'I will sell the buffaloes,' said Krishan, adding rather cheekily: 'Perhaps you will buy one of them, Subedar Sahib!'

He took the cheek out of his remark by adding 'Subedar-Sahib', the rank of a non-commissioned officer in the old Army. Hukam Singh, who had never reached this rank, was naturally flattered.

'Fortunately, Phambiri hasn't been to school! He'll be a farmer, and a fine one too.'

Phambiri simply grunted, which could have meant anything. He hadn't studied further than class six, which was just as well, as he was a man of muscle, not brain.

Phambiri loved putting his strength to some practical and useful purpose. Whenever the cartwheels got stuck in the mud, he would get off, remove his shirt, and put his shoulder to the side of the cart, while his muscles bulged and the sweat glistened on his broad back.

'Phambiri is the strongest man in our district,' said Hukum Singh proudly. 'And clever, too! It takes quick thinking to win a wrestling match.'

'I have never seen one,' said Sita.

'Then stay with us tomorrow morning, and you will see Phambiri wrestle. He has been challenged by the Karauli champion. It will be a great fight!'

'We must see Phambiri win,' said Krishan.

'Will there be time?' asked Sita.

'Why not? The train for Shahganj won't come in till evening. The fair goes on all day, and the wrestling bouts will take place in the morning.'

'Yes, you must see me win!' exclaimed Phambiri, thumping

himself on the chest as he climbed back on to the cart after freeing the wheels. 'No one can defeat me!'

'How can you be so certain?' asked Krishan.

'He *has* to be certain,' said Hukam Singh. 'I have taught him to be certain! You can't win anything if you are uncertain… Isn't that right, Phambiri? You *know* you are going to win!'

'I know,' said Phambiri, with a grunt of confidence.

'Well, someone has to lose,' said Krishan.

'Very true,' said Hukam Singh smugly. 'After all, what would we do without losers? But for Phambiri, it is win, win, all the time!'

'And *if* he loses?' persisted Krishan.

'Then he will just forget that it happened, and will go on to win his next fight!'

Krishan found Hukam Singh's logic almost unanswerable, but Sita, who had been puzzled by the argument, now saw everything very clearly and said, 'Perhaps he hasn't won any fights as yet. Did he lose the last one?'

'Hush!' said Hukam Singh, looking alarmed. 'You must not let him remember. You do not remember losing a fight, do you, my son?'

'I have never lost a fight,' said Phambiri with great simplicity and confidence.

'How strange,' said Sita. 'If you lose, how can you win?'

'Only a soldier can explain that,' said Hukam Singh. 'For a man who fights, there is no such thing as defeat. You fought against the river, did you not?'

'I went with the river,' said Sita. 'I went where it took me.'

'Yes, and you would have gone to the bottom if the boy had not come along to help you. He fought the river, didn't he?'

'Yes, he fought the river,' said Sita.

'You helped me to fight it,' said Krishan.

'So you both fought,' said the old man with a nod of satisfaction. 'You did not go with the river. You did not leave everything to the gods.'

'The gods were with us,' said Sita.

And so they talked, while the bullock-cart trundled along the muddy village roads. Both bullocks were white, and were decked out for the fair with coloured beaded necklaces and bells hanging from their necks. They were patient, docile beasts. But the cartwheels; which were badly in need of oiling, protested loudly, creaking and groaning as though all the demons in the world had been trapped within them.

Sita noticed a number of birds in the paddy fields. There were black and white curlews, and cranes with pink coat-tails. A good monsoon means plenty of birds. But Hukam Singh was not happy about the cranes.

'They do great damage in the wheat fields,' he said. Lighting up a small hand-held hookah pipe, he puffed at it and became philosophical again: 'Life is one long struggle for the farmer. When he has overcome the drought, survived the flood, hunted off the pig, killed the crane, and reaped the crop, then comes that bloodsucking ghoul, the moneylender. There is no escaping him! Is your father in debt to a moneylender, boy?'

'No,' said Krishan.

'That is because he doesn't have daughters who must be married! I have two. As they resemble Phambiri, they will need generous dowries.'

In spite of his grumbling, Hukam Singh seemed fairly content with his lot. He'd had a good maize crop, and the front of his cart was piled high with corn. He would sell the crop at the fair, along with some cucumbers, eggplants and melons.

The bad road had slowed them down so much that when darkness came they were still far from Karauli. In India there is hardly any twilight. Within a short time of the sun's going down, the stars were out.

'Six miles to go,' said Hukam Singh. 'In the dark our wheels may get stuck again. Let us spend the night here. If it rains, we can pull an old tarpaulin over the cart.'

Krishan made a fire in the charcoal burner which Hukam Singh had brought along, and they had a simple meal, roasting the corn over the fire and flavouring it with salt and spices and a squeeze of lemon. There was some milk, but not enough for everyone because Phambiri drank three tumblers by himself.

'If I win tomorrow,' he said, 'I will give all of you a feast!'

They settled down to sleep in the bullock-cart, and Phambiri and his father were soon snoring. Krishan lay awake, his arms crossed behind his head, staring up at the stars. Sita was very tired but she couldn't sleep. She was worrying about her grandparents, and wondering when she would see them again.

The night was full of sounds. The loud snoring that came from Phambiri and his father seemed to be taken up by invisible sleepers all around them, and Sita, becoming alarmed, turned to Krishan and asked, 'What is that strange noise?'

He smiled in the darkness, and she could see his white teeth and the glint of laughter in his eyes.

'Only the spirits of lost demons,' he said, and then laughed. 'Can't you recognize the music of the frogs?'

And that was what they heard—a sound more hideous

than the wail of demons, a rising crescendo of noise—*wurrk, wurrk, wurrk*—coming from the flooded ditches on either side of the road. All the frogs in the jungle seemed to have gathered at that one spot, and each one appeared to have something to say for himself. The speeches continued for about an hour. Then the meeting broke up, and silence returned to the forest.

A jackal slunk across the road. A puff of wind brushed through the trees. The bullocks, freed from the cart, were asleep beside it. The men's snores were softer now. Krishan slept, a half smile on his face. Only Sita lay awake, worried and waiting for the dawn.

At the Fair

Already, at nine o' clock, the fairground was crowded. Cattle were being sold or auctioned. Stalls had opened, selling everything from pins to ploughs. Foodstuffs were on sale—hot food, spicy food, sweets and ices. A merry-go-round, badly oiled, was squeaking and groaning, while a loudspeaker blared popular film music across the grounds.

While Phambiri was preparing for his wrestling match, Hukam Singh was busy haggling over the price of pumpkins. Sita and Krishan wandered on their own among the stalls, gazing at toys and kites and bangles and clothing, at brightly coloured, syrupy sweets. Some of the rural people had transistor-radios dangling by straps from their shoulders, the radio music competing with the loudspeaker. Occasionally a buffalo bellowed, drowning all other sounds.

Various people were engaged in roadside professions.

There was the fortune-teller. He had slips of paper, each of them covered with writing, which he kept in little trays along with some grain. He had a tame sparrow. When you gave the fortune-teller your money, he allowed the little bird to hop in and out among the trays until it stopped at one and started pecking at the grain. From this tray the fortune-teller took the slip of paper and presented it to his client. The writing told you what to expect over the next few months or years.

A harassed, middle aged man, who was surrounded by six noisy sons and daughters, was looking a little concerned, because his slip of paper said: 'Do not lose hope. You will have a child soon.'

Some distance away sat a barber, and near him a professional ear-cleaner. Several children clustered around a peepshow, which was built into an old gramophone cabinet. While one man wound up the gramophone and placed a well-worn record on the turntable, his partner pushed coloured pictures through a slide-viewer.

A young man walked energetically up and down the fairground, beating a drum and announcing the day's attractions. The wrestling bouts were about to start. The main attraction was going to be the fight between Phambiri, described as a man 'whose thighs had the thickness of an elephant's trunk', and the local champion, Sher Dil ('Tiger's Heart')—a wild-looking man, with hairy chest and beetling brow. He was heavier than Phambiri but not so tall. Sita and Krishan joined Hukam Singh at one corner of the akhara, the wrestling-pit. Hukam Singh was massaging his son's famous thighs.

A gong sounded and Sher Dil entered the ring, slapping himself on the chest and grunting like a wild boar. Phambiri advanced slowly to meet him.

They came to grips immediately, and stood swaying from side to side, two giants pitting their strength against each other. The sweat glistened on their well-oiled bodies.

Sher Dil got his arms round Phambiri's waist and tried to lift him off his feet; but Phambiri had twined one powerful leg around his opponent's thigh, and they both came down together with a loud squelch, churning up the soft mud of the wrestling-pit. But neither wrestler had been pinned down.

Soon they were so covered with mud that it was difficult to distinguish one from the other. There was a flurry of arms and legs. The crowd was cheering, and Sita and Krishan were cheering too, but the wrestlers were too absorbed in their struggle to be aware of their supporters. Each sought to turn the other on to his back. That was all that mattered. There was no count.

For a few moments Sher Dil had Phambiri almost helpless, but Phambiri wriggled out of a crushing grip and, using his legs once again, sent Sher Dil rocketing across the akhara. But Sher Dil landed on his belly, and even with Phambiri on top of him, it wasn't victory.

Nothing happened for several minutes, and the crowd became restless and shouted for more action. Phambiri thought of twisting his opponent's ear; but he realized that he might get disqualified for doing that, so he restrained himself. He relaxed his grip slightly, and this gave Sher Dil a chance to heave himself up and sent Phambiri spinning across the akhara. Phambiri was still in a sitting position when the other took a flying leap at him. But Phambiri dived forward, taking his opponent between the legs, and then rising, flung him backwards with a resounding thud. Sher Dil was helpless, and Phambiri sat on his opponent's chest to remove all doubts as to who was the winner. Only when the applause of the spectators told him that he had won did he rise and leave the ring.

Accompanied by his proud father, Phambiri accepted the prize money, thirty rupees, and then went in search of a tap. After he had washed the oil and mud from his body, he put on fresh clothes. Then, putting his arms around Krishan and Sita, he said, 'You have brought me luck, both of you. Now let us celebrate!' And he led the way to the sweet shops.

They ate syrupy rasgullas (made from milk and sugar) and almond-filled fudge, and little pies filled with minced meat, and washed everything down with a fizzy orange drink.

'Now I will buy each of you a small present,' said Phambiri.

He bought a bright blue sports shirt for Krishan. He bought a new hookah bowl for his father. And he took Sita to a stall where dolls were sold, and asked her to choose one.

There were all kinds of dolls—cheap plastic dolls, and beautiful dolls made by hand, dressed in the traditional costumes of different regions of the country. Sita was immediately reminded of Mumta, her own rag doll, who had been made at home with Grandmother's help. And she remembered Grandmother, and Grandmother's sewing machine, and the home that had been swept away, and the tears started to roll down her eyes.

The dolls seemed to smile at Sita. The shopkeeper held them up one by one, and they appeared to dance, to twirl their wide skirts, to stamp their jingling feet on the counter. Each doll had its own special appeal to Sita. Each one wanted her love.

'Which one will you have?' asked Phambiri. 'Choose the prettiest, never mind the price!'

But Sita could say nothing, she could only shake her head. No doll, no matter how beautiful, could replace Mumta. She would never keep a doll again. That part of her life was over.

So instead of a doll Phambiri bought her coloured glass bangles which slipped easily over Sita's thin wrists. And then he took them into a temporary cinema, a large shed made of corrugated tin sheets.

Krishan had been in a cinema before—the towns were full of cinemas—but for Sita it was another new experience. Many things that were common enough for other boys and girls were strange and new for a girl who had spent nearly all her life on a small island in the middle of a big river.

As they found seats, a curtain rolled up and a white sheet came into view. A babble of talk dwindled into silence. Sita became aware of a whirring noise somewhere not far behind her; but, before she could turn her head to see what it was, the sheet became a rectangle of light and colour. It came to life. People moved and spoke. A story unfolded.

But, long afterwards, all that Sita could remember of her first film was a jumble of images and incidents. A train in danger: the audience murmuring with anxiety: a bridge over a river (but a smaller than hers): the bridge being blown to pieces: the engine plunging into the river: people struggling in the water: a woman rescued by a man who immediately embraced her: the lights coming on again, and the audience rising slowly and drifting out of the theatre, looking quite unconcerned and even satisfied. All those people struggling in the water were now quite safe, back in the little black box in the projection room.

Catching the Train

And now a real engine, a steam engine belching smoke and fire, was on its way to Sita.

She stood with Krishan on the station platform along with over a hundred other people waiting for the Shahganj train.

The platform was littered with the familiar bedrolls (or holdalls) without which few people in India ever travel. On these rolls sat women, children, great-aunts and great-uncles, grandfathers, grandmothers and grandchildren, while the more active adults hovered at the edge of the platform, ready to leap onto the train as soon as it arrived and reserve a space for the family. In India, people do not travel alone if they can help it. The whole family must be taken along—especially if the reason for the journey is a marriage, a pilgrimage, or simply a visit to friends or relations.

Moving among the piles of bedding and luggage were coolies, vendors of magazines, sweetmeats, tea and betel-leaf preparations. The cries of the vendors mingled with the general clamour of the station and the shunting of a steam engine in the yards.

But there came the train!

The signal was down. The crowd surged forward, swamping an assistant stationmaster. Krishan took Sita by the hand and led her forward. If they were too slow, they would not get a place on the crowded train. In front of them was a tall, burly, bearded Sikh from Punjab. Krishan decided it would be a wise move to stand behind him and move forward at the same time.

Krishan stayed closed to the Sikh who forged a way through the throng. The Sikh reached an open doorway and was through. Krishan and Sita were through! They found somewhere to sit, and were then able to look down at the platform, into the whirlpool, and enjoy themselves a little. The vendors had abandoned the people on the platform and had started selling their wares at the windows. Hukam Singh, after buying their tickets, had given Krishan and Sita a rupee to spend on the way. Krishan bought a freshly split coconut, and Sita bought a comb for her disarranged hair. She had never bothered with her hair before.

They saw a worried man rushing along the platform searching for his family; but they were already in the compartment, having beaten him to it, and eagerly helped him in at the door. A whistle shrilled, and they were off! A couple of vendors made last-minute transactions, then jumped from the slow-moving train. One man did this expertly with a tray of teacups balanced on one hand.

The train gathered speed.

'What will happen to all those people still on the platform?' asked Sita anxiously. 'Will they all be left behind?'

She put her head out of the window and looked back at the receding platform. It was strangely empty. Only the vendors and the coolies and the stray dogs and the dishevelled railway staff were in evidence. A miracle had happened. No one—absolutely no one—had been left behind!

Then the train was rushing through the night, the engine throwing out bright sparks that danced away like fireflies. Sometimes the train had to slow down, as floodwater had weakened the embankments. Sometimes it stopped at brightly lit stations.

When the train started again and moved on into the dark countryside, Sita would stare through the glass of the window, at the bright lights of a town or the quiet glow of village lamps. She thought of Phambiri and Hukam Singh, and wondered if she would ever see them again. Already they were like people in a fairy tale, met briefly on the road and never seen again.

There was no room in the compartment in which to lie down; but Sita soon fell asleep, her head resting against Krishan's shoulder.

A Meeting and a Parting

Sita did not know where to look for Grandfather. For an hour, she and Krishan wandered through the Shahganj bazaar, growing hungrier all the time. They had no money left, and they were hot and thirsty.

Outside the bazaar, near a small temple, they saw a tree in which several small boys were helping themselves to the sour, purple fruit.

It did not take Krishan long to join the boys in the tree. They did not object to his joining them. It wasn't their tree, anyway.

Sita stood beneath the tree, while Krishan threw the jamuns down to her. They soon had a small pile of the fruit. They were on the road again, their faces stained with purple juice.

They were asking the way to the Shahganj hospital when Sita caught a glimpse of her grandfather on the road.

At first the old man did not recognize her. He was walking stiffly down the road, looking straight ahead, and would have walked right past the dusty, dishevelled girl, had she not charged straight at his thin, shaky legs and clasped him round the waist.

'Sita!' he cried, when he had recovered his wind and his balance. 'Why are you here? How did you get off the island? I have been very worried—it has been bad, these last two days...'

'Is Grandmother all right?' asked Sita.

But even as she spoke, she knew that Grandmother was no longer with them. The dazed look in the old man's eyes told her as much. She wanted to cry—not for Grandmother, who could suffer no more, but for Grandfather, who looked so helpless and bewildered; she did not want him to be unhappy. She forced back her tears, and took his gnarled and trembling hand; and, with Krishan walking beside her, led the old man down the crowded street.

She knew, then, that it would be on her shoulder that Grandfather would lean on in the years to come.

They decided to remain in Shahganj for a couple of days, staying at a dharamsala—a wayside rest-house—until the floodwaters subsided. Grandfather still had two of the goats—it had not been necessary to sell more than one—but he did not want to take the risk of rowing a crowded boat across to the island. The river was still fast and dangerous.

But Krishan could not stay with Sita any longer.

'I must go now,' he said. 'My father and mother will be very worried, and they will not know where to look for me. In a day or two the water will go down, and you will be able to go back to your home.'

'Perhaps the island has gone forever,' said Sita.

'It will be there,' said Krishan. 'It is a rocky island. Bad for crops, but good for a house!'

'Will you come?' asked Sita.

What she really wanted to say was, 'Will you come to see me?' but she was too shy to say it; and besides, she wasn't sure if Krishan would want to see her again.

'I will come,' said Krishan. 'That is, if my father gets me another boat!'

As he turned to go, he gave her his flute.

'Keep it for me,' he said. 'I will come for it one day.'

When he saw her hesitate, he smiled and said, 'It is a good flute!'

The Return

There was more rain, but the worst was over, and when Grandfather and Sita returned to the island, the river was no longer in spate.

Grandfather could hardly believe his eyes when he saw that the tree had disappeared—the tree that had seemed as permanent as the island, as much a part of his life as the river itself had been. He marvelled at Sita's escape.

'It was the tree that saved you,' he said.

'And the boy,' said Sita.

'Yes, and the boy.'

She thought about Krishan and wondered if she would ever see him again. Would he, like Phambiri and Hukam Singh, be one of those people who arrived as though out of a fairy tale and then disappeared silently and mysteriously? She did not know it then, but some of the moving forces of our lives are meant to touch us briefly and go their way...

And because Grandmother was no longer with them, life on the island was quite different. The evenings were sad and lonely.

But there was a lot of work to be done, and Sita did not have much time to think of Grandmother or Krishan or the world she had glimpsed during her journey.

For three nights they slept under a crude shelter made out of gunny-bags. During the day Sita helped Grandfather rebuild the mud hut. Once again, they used the big rock for support.

The trunk which Sita had packed so carefully had not been swept off the island, but the water had got into it, and the food and clothing had been spoilt. But Grandfather's hookah had been saved, and, in the evenings after work was done and they had eaten their light meal which Sita prepared, he would smoke with a little of his old contentment, and tell Sita about other floods which he had experienced as a boy. And he would tell her about the wrestling matches he had won, and the kites he had flown, for he remembered a time when grown men flew kites, and great battles were fought, the kites swooping and swerving in the sky, tangling with each other until the string of one was cut.

Kite-flying was then the sport of kings, Grandfather remembered how the Raja himself would come down to the riverbank and join in this noble pastime. There was time in those days to spend an hour with a gay, dancing strip of paper. Now everyone hurried, in a heat of hope, and delicate things like kites and daydreams were trampled underfoot.

Grandfather remembered the 'Dragon Kite' that he had

built—a great kite with a face painted on it, the eyes made of small mirrors, the tail like a long crawling serpent. A large crowd assembled to watch its launching. At the first attempt it refused to leave the ground. And then the wind came from the right direction, and the Dragon Kite soared into the sky, wriggling its way higher and higher, with the sun still glinting in its eyes. And it went very high, it pulled fiercely on the twine determined to be free, to break loose, to live a life of its own. And eventually it did.

The twine snapped, the kite leapt away toward the sun, sailed on heavenward until it was lost to view. It was never found again, and Grandfather wondered if he had made too vivid, too living a thing of the great kite. He did not make another like it.

It was like her doll, thought Sita.

Mumta had been a real person, not a doll, and now Sita could not make another like her.

Sita planted a mango seed in the same spot where the peepul tree had stood. It would be many years before it grew into a big tree, but Sita liked to imagine sitting in the branches one day, picking the mangoes straight from the tree and feasting on them all day.

Grandfather was more particular about making a vegetable garden, putting down peas, carrots, gram and mustard.

One day, when most of the hard work had been done and the new hut was ready, Sita took the flute which had been given to her by Krishan, and walked down to the water's edge and tried to play it. But all she could produce was a few broken notes, and even the goats paid no attention to her music.

Sometimes Sita thought she saw a boat coming down the

river, and she would run to meet it; but usually there was no boat, or, if there was, it belonged to a stranger or to another fisherman. And so she stopped looking out for boats.

Slowly, the rains came to an end. The floodwaters had receded, and in the villages people were beginning to till the land again and sow crops for the winter months. There were more cattle fairs and wrestling matches. The days were warm and sultry. The water in the river was no longer muddy, and one evening Grandfather brought home a huge mahseer fish, and Sita made it into a delicious curry.

Deep River

Grandfather sat outside the hut, smoking his hookah. Sita was at the far end of the island, spreading clothes on the rocks to dry. One of the goats had followed her. It was the friendlier of the two and often followed Sita about the island. She had made it a necklace of coloured beads.

She sat down on a smooth rock, and, as she did so, she noticed a small bright object in the sand near her feet. She picked it up. It was a little wooden toy—a coloured peacock, Lord Krishna's favourite bird—it must have come down on the river and been swept ashore on the island. Some of the paint had been rubbed off; but for Sita, who had no toys, it was a great find.

There was a soft footfall behind her. She looked round, and there was Krishan, barefooted, standing over her and smiling.

'I thought you wouldn't come,' said Sita.

'There was much work in my village. Did you keep my flute?' 'Yes, but I cannot play it properly.'

'I will teach you,' said Krishan.

He sat down beside her, and they cooled their feet in the water, which was clear now, taking in the blue of the sky. You could see the sand and the pebbles of the river-bed.

'Sometimes the river is angry and sometimes it is kind,' said Sita. 'We are part of the river,' said Krishan.

◆

It was a good river, deep and strong, beginning in the mountains and ending in the sea.

Along its banks, for hundreds of miles, lived millions of people, and Sita was only one small girl among them, and no one had ever heard of her, no one knew her—except for the old man, and the boy, and the water that was blue and white and wonderful.